# Imperfect Vengeance

## By

## A.S. Matthews

*Thanks to Maureen, Sue, Vivian, Jean, Aunt Sarah, my sister Rene, and my Mom Elaine and her book club for their help and support with the book!*

978-0-557-70692-1

# Chapter 1

Blytheville is a small town in the central part of Arkansas, population 12,000. There's one elementary, one middle and one high school. It's hard not to know everyone around you and everything about them. Ellen Jacobs is the exception. Ellen is a quiet girl; some think she is a bit slow. Her family moved to Blytheville from Tennessee when she was 15 and she has had a difficult time with the move. She doesn't engage much with the other kids, always feeling like an outsider. Not many people choose Blytheville as a new home so she is one of the few new children in the school system, especially high school. She left behind several close friends back in Tennessee and she misses them terribly. They have no money for her to call or keep in touch with them so she writes when she can. At least she has her family.

Ellen lacks the interpersonal skills needed to penetrate this new environment. The children horrify her. They tease her every day—the way she speaks, the way she dresses, the backpack she carries. She can never quite understand why they enjoy torturing her so much. It's not like she chose to move to Blytheville. She lives with her family in a beaten-up old house on a farm on the outskirts of town, walking to school every day on a dirt path and through a section of woods. Her father, Joe, works on the farm and sells soybeans.

They moved to Blytheville after Ellen's mom died from cancer. It was a very painful death and Ellen spent as much time as possible trying to care for her mother. She loved her mother and was devastated when she died. Remaining in Tennessee surrounded by his wife's family was too hard for Joe so he moved the family. He knew it would be difficult raising children without help but he was depressed and just needed to escape.

Ellen is not an un-attractive girl, her hair "dirty" blonde. The "dirty" is in color as well as condition. She wears her hair down every day, the sides hanging to cover her face from others. Every day Ellen puts on a beat-up old red and black plaid jacket which is frayed at the ends, and faded jeans. The jacket is always closed tightly around her, even in the summer. She is of moderate height, and has green eyes with a faraway look in a plain round face. Her skin is very pale, as if she hasn't seen the sun one day in her life! When you look at Ellen you get the sense of desperation, of someone trying to hold on to the last fragment of hope.

Cyrus and his friends John and Mike are sitting on the Balasky Bridge. They should be in school but Cyrus convinces them to ditch the last two classes and get stoned. They are 18 and about to graduate from high school. Mike is a young man, 18, but nearly a head taller than the other boys. He is slim but in very good shape, with the body of a true athlete. He has a hard face for such a young boy; a full beard makes him look quite a bit older. His eyes are empty and brown. He seldom smiles. Growing up in Blytheville is something he is hoping to soon forget. Freshman and sophomore girls follow him around school like little puppy dogs just waiting for a pat. He is the quarterback of the high school football team, and has made all state three years in a row. A

4

couple more weeks and he will be on his way, full ride to a school of his choice.

The boys are killing time, talking about what they are going to do when they get out of Blytheville when they see Ellen coming. She is walking home from school alone, deep in her own thoughts. In her fiction class today she got back the short story she wrote about a young adolescent girl falling in love for the first time. She really enjoyed writing the story; it enabled her to daydream about what life must be like for girls other than her. She mirrored the character to herself, but made her much more attractive and popular. The young boy she falls in love with is an exceptional athlete, homecoming king. It is a real Cinderella story, but what makes it so special is the passion she puts into her writing. The grade...an A! She can't wait to get home and show her father. She rushes home, forgetting to pick up her younger sister and brother.

She walks quickly with a slight smile on her face, looking out over the water. Her normally blank eyes actually have a sparkle today. Her peaceful walk is suddenly cut short when she notices the boys on the bridge. As she approaches them she tightens her grip on her backpack and begins to walk faster. She knows they are going to tease her, like everyone else does. She can feel the hairs on her neck standing up, preparing for the verbal attack. She starts to walk faster as she crosses to the other side of the bridge. Mike watches her closely. As he sees her cross the road, he leans over to Cyrus,

"Hey, take a look at the freak!"

Cyrus just laughs and yells, "Hey freak! Where you going?" They all laugh.

Ellen just stiffens up and walks faster. "Here we go," she says to herself.

John is the first to get up and lean against the bridge rail. Then Cyrus and Mike follow.

"Hey, he asked you a question! Where you going?" yells Mike.

Cyrus starts to edge his way into the road yelling again, "Hey freak! We just want to talk to you."

Ellen starts to panic and begins to walk/run. The tone in their voice is scaring her. They are making her really nervous.

John sees Cyrus move into the road and says, "Cyrus, where you going?"

Cyrus says, "I'm just gonna go talk to her, get a closer look. Right, Mike?"

Mike agrees and moves into the road with Cyrus.

The boys move quickly to catch up to Ellen and keep pace behind her.

Cyrus keeps going with his harassing comments, "Freak, slow down. We just want to talk to you."

The boys surround Ellen, pushing her with their shoulders. She lets out only slight noises, quickly making them aware of how scared she is. This only adds to their pleasure and excitement.

Cyrus turns to John and says, "Hey man, I think she was checking you out back there. She must want to be 'friends' with you." He laughs after he says it. John just looks at Cyrus with complete confusion. John doesn't know what they are doing.

Mike chimes in, "Ellen, you like John? Because if you do, we can leave you two alone for a while. What do you think about that John?"

Ellen starts to cry loudly.

Mike says, "Oh you don't need to cry. Look, John, she's so happy she's crying. Cyrus, let's leave the lovebirds alone!"

Cyrus quickly replies, "Why should John have all the fun? Maybe we can all be 'friends'." He has an evil laugh this time and pushes Ellen off the road. She stumbles a bit and then starts to run in a total panic, screaming.

Thoughts are running through her head, "Oh my God, what am I gonna do? Where can I go? Can anyone hear me screaming?"

They run a few hundred yards off the road into the trees. They are all sweating from the heat, Ellen is fast. She throws her backpack down as she weaves through the trees, jumping over obstacles in her path. She is crying loudly now in sheer fright. The boys are all around her, playing with her, pushing at her. She doesn't understand what is going on. Why today? Why her?

The trees are huge oaks with large green leaves; they don't allow for a lot of light. It's the middle of the afternoon but if feels like dusk. Mixed into the oaks are large Douglas firs. The needles prick Ellen's arms as she runs through them. In between the trees are several trails carved by kids on motorcycles and ATVs. The trails are muddy because they don't get enough sun to stay dry. It takes several weeks after a rain for the ground to dry. The air is damp and warm, very muggy from the rain the day before. It is like the oxygen is being pushed to the ground by the moisture in the air. Ellen is struggling to keep her breath as she runs through the trees. She can hear echoes of the boys' laughter as they shout from behind her. With each step she takes she feels them getting closer and closer. Her heart is pounding so hard and fast she thinks it will come out of her chest. She is losing her footing on the trail; the mud is slippery and thick. She's getting tired, running on pure adrenalin. She desperately tries to keep herself moving forward, pleading with herself not to fall.

Crazy thoughts are running through her head as she runs. What made today different? Has she done something to attract their attention, said the wrong thing in class. Did she give an unsuspecting glance or smile their way? All of these things beat through Ellen's head as she runs for her life through the blistering woods. She runs and runs until she finally loses her footing. As she lies in the rough, muddy ground, leaves falling down on her sweaty face, Ellen eerily makes peace with what is about to happen. As the boys run up and surround her, all she can hear is their muffled voices, as if she has risen above the horrific scene and floated into the air.

She feels as if she is in a fog, but she is quickly jolted out of it when the boys begin to paw at her. She looks up to see large smirks on their faces and hear their laughter. They are shrieking like a pack of coyotes. Ellen is numb but she tries to fight back. She fights as hard as she can, her cries echoing against the dark, solemn woods. One of the boys pins her arms down while the other braces her legs. Ellen can no longer move.

Mike says, "Ellen, what's wrong? We just want to talk to you! What are you afraid of?" Ellen turns away.

Cyrus sneers, "She must not like the way we smell man! What do you think, the freak doesn't like the way we smell, huh freak!"

Ellen continues to weep softly. Cyrus's grasp is strong. His big hands around her neck are much too much for feeble Ellen to take. She starts to choke.

"Look who's not talking now," says Cyrus.

John says, "Cyrus, what are you doing? You're gonna hurt her man! I thought you just wanted to have some fun with her."

John isn't a lady's man by any means; women actually scare him. He feels sorry for Ellen. He remembers when she came to Blytheville and how alienated everyone made her feel. He knows what that feels like. He is good friends with Mike and Cyrus but only because he fears them more than likes them. He has always felt out of place but he knows if he doesn't find some group to join he will be, well, just like Ellen.

Mike says, "This is fun man, what's wrong with you. Don't you want see what the freak's always hiding behind the jacket?"

Ellen lay there unconscious.

Cyrus quickly reaches down and starts tearing her jacket away from her saying, "Yeah man, I want to see what's under the jacket! What are you hiding in here freak?"

Ellen wakes and screams out; she can't believe what is happening. She is completely bewildered! She is lying on the cold ground disrobed from the waist up. Then Mike chimes in and proceeds to undo her pants. With a quick jerk of her body, Mike scratches her stomach. She starts to fight back like a wild cat, completely unaware of how far they have pushed her. She is on her back and then on her stomach. She tosses around onto her knees and then to her feet. She is completely covered in mud and bloody scratches. She starts to kick and punch, scratch and claw, getting Cyrus's face first.

He yells in pain, "You bitch, you scratched me," and then punches Ellen in the face. She flies back, hitting her head hard on a rock.

John screams, "Cyrus what are you doing?"

Cyrus turns and says, "The bitch scratched me man. I'm gonna fuck her first!" Cyrus is completely enraged.

Mike is right next to him, still pulling at her pants, "Yeah and then I'm next man. This bitch kicked me in the nuts."

John can't believe it. What is wrong with these guys?

As Cyrus mounts poor Ellen, he notices she is not moving. He grabs her face, "listen bitch", Cyrus says. And as he turns her face toward his Ellen's eyes just stare blankly at him. That glimmer she had earlier has completely faded. Cyrus freaks out and quickly dismounts Ellen. "What the fuck," he says. "Fuck, fuck." Cyrus stands up. The other two are standing around her, all looking down on Ellen's lifeless body.

John says with tears in his eyes, "I think you guys killed her."

Mike moves in to make sure she isn't faking. He pokes at her, "Hey freak. get up, freak!" Ellen doesn't move. Mike leans forward to feel her pulse and he doesn't feel anything, "I think John's right man, she ain't breathing!"

Cyrus says, "Well I'm still gonna fuck her!" Cyrus climbs on top of her and enters her.

John stands there watching in shock. He is mortified. These guys he thought are decent, that he calls friends, are nothing but losers and now rapists and murderers. John tries to keep his cool. These guys are so hyped up, he thought, if he makes a scene he will be next.

When Cyrus is finished, Mike takes his turn.

Mike and Cyrus, both finished, they put on their pants, wipe the sweat off their faces and say, "Your turn. John boy".

John looks disgusted. "No way, man, I ain't fucking a corpse."

Cyrus gets up in his face, "C'mon man, we're all in this thing together. You fuck her or you'll end up like her."

Mike starts howling with laughter. "Yeah man, we're all in this together bro."

Mike and Cyrus stand there with the look of the devil in them. John slowly undoes his belt and drops his pants. As he climbs on top of Ellen's cold body he vomits. He can't get an erection. He lies there on top of her and starts to cry.

"You fucking sissy," says Cyrus.

"Yeah, sissy," Mike says. "Come on man, let's get out of here. Put your pants back on, man.

Cyrus turns to John, "Man, you say a word and you know what's gonna happen! You understand? You better just keep your mouth shut.

Now let's get out of here! I gotta get home before my Dad gets home from work."

As they turn to leave, John looks back and stops. He grabs Ellen's jacket and covers her body up with it. He can't believe what has happened. As he's lying the jacket over her body he hears a branch snap. He turns to look at Cyrus and Mike but they are standing still, waiting for him. He quickly looks around to see if he can spot where the noise came from but he doesn't see anything.

"Did you guys' here that?" He asks Mike and Cyrus.

"Hear what? The sound of you whining." Cyrus snips.

"No man, I heard a noise. I think someone's out there." John says in a loud whisper.

"There's nobody out there John, let's go." Mike says.

John looks around again. He knows what he heard. He slowly stands up from Ellen's body, not looking down, and starts to walk backwards toward Mike and Cyrus backwards. He can't see anyone but he feels it. He puts his head down and turns to follow Mike and Cyrus back to the bridge.

# Chapter 2

The next morning Cyrus wakes up. He has hardly slept and his face hurts. He goes into the kitchen. His mom is in the kitchen making breakfast for his little sister, Bonnie. She is a younger woman, but time hasn't been good to Mary. She has a hard time of it, raising two kids by herself. Her husband walked out on her when he found out she was pregnant with Cyrus's sister. One accident he could handle. but two, that was just too many mouths to feed.

Mary had to find a way to support them so she works two jobs. She works at Vicky's Salon as a manicurist by day and a stripper by night. She glances over at Cyrus as he enters, notices his face but doesn't care enough to ask. She just assumes he was in a fight; he is always looking for trouble.

"Good morning," Mary says. Cyrus just grumbles.

"You need to clean up the garage when you get home. I've got to work late tonight."

"Yeah, alright," Cyrus mumbles.

"I mean it Cyrus. Don't forget. I can't even walk through the garage there's so much crap all over the place." She says as she puts some toast on a plate.

"Alright, I said I would do it. Man."

"Yeah, just like you were gonna clean up your room yesterday. Just like you're gonna do everything...you never do nothing."

Cyrus just grabs a piece of toast from his sister's plate.

"Cy!" Bonnie snaps. "You're a jerk."

"What, I'm hungry." He says as he gets up from the table.

As he picks up his backpack he sees the newspaper on the counter and wonders if it's in the paper. He starts flipping through the pages but there is nothing. No story of rape and no story of a murdered girl. He knew it, she was faking. She isn't dead. John didn't know what he was talking about.

He's gonna give John shit when he gets to school today. Cyrus eats a piece of toast and drinks some orange juice, grabs his bag and heads out.

Bonnie yells, "Hey wait for me Cy. I thought you were gonna drop me off at school today."

Cyrus yells back, "Well, then get off your ass and let's go."

Bonnie gets up quickly, grabbing a piece of toast on her way out. "Bye Mom, love you."

Bonnie is a pretty little girl, only 12 but starting to develop into quite a curvy little woman. She has curly brown hair and beautiful blue eyes. She isn't too tall, 5'1", and loves to wear colorful, coordinated clothing. It really shows off her eyes. She doesn't look anything like Cyrus. Cyrus is blonde with blue eyes. He is tall and slender, some will even say skinny. He has terrible acne, which he attempts to hide with stubble on his face. His teeth are in need of braces, which his family could never afford. He hunches over all the time because he lacks self-confidence. He dresses like he has no home in torn and unwashed t-shirts, but he doesn't care. Appearance means nothing to Cyrus.

As they drive off to school in Cyrus's '79 Chevy Nova, he is happier and more pleasant that normal. Bonnie asks him to what she owes this pleasant disposition.

Cyrus snips, "What do you care? Just get in the car and shut up."

They drive through a residential area, each house different, yet something about them feels the same. Maybe it is the families that live in each house or maybe it is neighborhood itself. Each house is a single family home with two stories and a square front lawn. Each lawn is well manicured with a sidewalk going through the center to the standard four-pane metal painted front door. There are shutters beside each window, painted to match the front door. Large, flowering trees line the street. The weather is nice today and the humidity is low.

As they get closer to the school, the number of children walking on the sidewalk increases. The kids who live closer to the school walk each day. Cyrus's family can't afford that luxury; they live on the outskirts of town.

As they drive to school Cyrus has a slight smile on his face, a smile that says he is quite pleased with himself. He got away with something and he feels good about it. What happened yesterday with Ellen has makes him feel excited and strong! He can't wait to get to school today. Bonnie doesn't push it; she knows he won't tell her anyway.

She stares out the car window thinking about Steve, the new boy who has caught her attention. He has only been at the school for a week but she can't stop thinking about him. He is adorable, brown hair and brown eyes. Steve is tall and well built. an athlete. He is baseball player, and from what she has learned, a good one. He is smart too, a straight A student who isn't embarrassed that he likes school. He is perfect!

That morning, John asks his parents if they saw anything on TV, anything interesting and they both tell him no. He is flipping through the channels quickly, searching for any news regarding Ellen. His twin sister Jill asks him what he means by "interesting" but he diverts her question by pointing out how nice she looks that morning. He grabs the paper on the table and starts quickly flipping through the pages. He is feverishly looking for any news, any information regarding Ellen. He is sure if something has happened to her it will be in the paper, on the news. There is nothing. He starts to feel relieved that maybe she is okay, maybe she isn't dead. If she is okay she hasn't said anything, or has she?

Mike doesn't even waste a minute of his morning looking through papers or turning on the TV. He wakes up; his mom and dad are still traveling on vacation in Napa Valley. His sister is staying at his aunt's; they don't really get along anyway, and he has the house all to himself. He is feeling no remorse; he is more concerned with whether or not he has gotten an STD from Ellen. Who knows where she has been.

Blytheville High School was built in 1965, made of faded red brick with white framed windows. The entrance to the school has double white doors with arched windows above the doors. The sign above the doors reads "Blytheville High School." There are two overgrown large trees in the front of the school on either side of the sidewalk leading up to the front doors. Groups of kids gather around the trees in an attempt to delay the inevitable start of the school day. Around the tree to the left are the kids who enjoy school and everything about it. They love to study and they hold all the school offices. The tree on the right is reserved for the jocks, their cheerleaders and other groupies. Each morning's conversations are about the weekend's parties and whatever mischief they managed to get into. Mike spends his days with his teammates but when he wants to ditch school and get in trouble he goes back to his childhood friends. There's less of a chance getting busted by the coach. Blytheville isn't a spiked hair, lots of chains and black clothing type of community, but there are a few students who enjoy punk rock. They paint their nails black and wear dark make-up around their eyes.

The parking lot is off to the left of the front entrance. The teachers park to the right. The school buses use the roadway in front of the entrance for pick-up and drop-off. There's a wanna-be policeman that patrols the road and anyone who tries to use the front road gets detention.

John and Cyrus are waiting out front for Mike when he gets to school. John can't believe there is nothing in the paper, he is sure Ellen is dead. He did feel a bit of relief though, to think they didn't kill her.

Mike walks up to Cyrus and John.

John says, "Man, did you notice the paper? I didn't see anything. She must be okay, right?"

Cyrus looks at John in anger, "Shut up man, someone may hear you. We can talk at lunch."

As they stand in front of the school, people pass by them as if in slow motion. Every glance, every eye contact causes them to wonder if they know. Did they see them chase Ellen into the woods? John is the most sensitive.

"Cy, I know I heard a noise in the woods. What if someone saw what we did?" John whispers.

"Shut it. John. You were so freaked out you were probably just hearing things." Cyrus snips.

"I don't think so." John replies as he studies every face walking past him. He thinks, "Did they tell someone and the police are waiting inside to talk to them, ask them questions about what they are doing?"

None of them can help but be paranoid. They can't have gotten away with it that easily, can they?

"Yeah, let's talk at lunch. I don't want to be late for Boilermaker's class. That dude needs some serious help; I mean, the toothbrush is not a new invention!" says Mike. He laughs as he starts to walk off to class.

John's in a daze through the morning classes. Sitting and staring at his desk, not making eye contact with anyone.

"John! I asked you what Presidency ended the Vietnam War. Aren't you listening?" Mrs. Peterson asked.

"What? I didn't hear the question Mrs. Peterson. I'm sorry. I'm not really feeling well today."

"Well then, stop and see the nurse before lunch and see if she can give you something."

"I will, Mrs. Peterson. Thanks." And he put his head back down, continuing to fret over the event.

John meets Mike and Cyrus for lunch in the cafeteria.

"I can't take this. I just can't do it." John says as they sit down to eat.

"John, you really need to chill, man. You're gonna get us caught." Mike quickly replies.

"I know, I know. You're right." He says looking around to see if anyone is watching. "I just can't stop thinking about it. I feel sick."

"Maybe you should go home, then." Cyrus says.

John thinks for a moment. "No, I can't go home. My mom'll ask me all kinds of questions. I've only got three more classes."

"Well, cut out the panic attacks, will ya?" Mike asks. "You're starting to make me freaked out." Now Mike has started looking around the cafeteria to see if anyone is watching. "I think we need to lay low for a few days, you know, no more hanging out at the bridge after school."

"You guys are crazy, man." Cyrus laughs.

"No, we're just not stoned like you, Cyrus." Mike says.

The tension only increases throughout the day for John and now Mike. When the school dismissal bell rings they rush out and each heads home.

Then next day John wakes up and flips through channels and the paper, in search of any information about Ellen. At school, Ellen isn't there again! As the hours tick by they wait for someone to come and pull

21

them out of class. Waiting to be questioned about Ellen and what they are doing in the woods. As each hour passes and no one shows up John gets more nervous.

John is sure it is only a matter of time. He is in the hall at his locker and he overhears a couple of kids talking about Ellen.

Hey Tina, I didn't see Ellen in creative writing class again today. Have you seen her?" Ted asks.

"Nope, haven't seen her. Maybe you should check with the office."

"Nah, I'm sure she'll be back tomorrow. Probably just sick. See you in Trig."

"Yeah, see ya."

They walk off to class and John's heart is racing. Kids are starting to ask questions, it's only a matter of time. He can't take it. He can't eat and he can't sleep. He knows they are going to get caught and when they do Cyrus will blame him. He and Mike will let John take the fall for it all. He doesn't want to go to jail.

John, not being able to resist because the silence is eating him up, takes off after school one day and walks out to her house. It is a beaten-up old ranch style house. The screens are falling off and the faded blue paint is weathered. There are a couple rusted pieces of farm equipment sitting to the side of the driveway. Around the back is a red barn and next to it are a few chickens and a goat pecking at what little grass is left. It is clear that the place has been abandoned. John shrugs his shoulders and wraps his arms around himself as a cold dust of wind gives him a chill.

He walks up to the dilapidated porch, trying to be careful not to fall through any of the holes. The door is ajar so John pushes it open, "Hello!" John calls out. No one replies.

His eerie feeling will not go away but he figures he has come this far, there is no turning back now. When he enters into the foyer he hears a crack and is startled! His heart is pounding and he is slightly out of breath as he quickly spins around the foyer and glimpses into each room. The dining room, living room and the foyer are all empty so John continues his search.

"Hello! Anyone home?" he says as he walks into the house. There is nothing in the room accept an old couch and a couple of tables. No pictures on the wall, no curtains, any books or knick knacks. What is going on? Where is everyone? He walks into the kitchen. The appliances are straight out of the '50s, with linoleum flooring, torn as if someone has dragged knives across the floor. There are a few dirty dishes in the sink and the faucet is dripping. He turns to go back out to the front door; there's is obviously no one in the house. It is like they moved out! Then it hits him. Maybe Ellen is alive but so ashamed that she moved? He sighs with relief at the thought of never having to face her. He can't bear it. He hasn't slept since the attack and doesn't think he is going to sleep anytime soon. He can't eat or focus on anything because he is so ridden with guilt.

John stands on the deserted front porch. A gust of wind blows through his hair. He closes his eyes and pictures Ellen alive and living somewhere else. He envisions Ellen's concerned father, holding his baby girl tight and telling her everything will be all right. They are on to a fresh new start where no one will hurt her.

John stands there his eyes still closed, visualizing his happy ending to such a terrifying ordeal. Then a loud bang comes from the barn. Startled, John opens his eyes. He walks over to the barn as thoughts of Ellen's father inside with a gun raced through head. His heart is pounding; it feels like all the blood in his body is rushing to his heart. This must be how Ellen felt when they were chasing her, but only worse.

John stands outside the barn door. He slowly opens the creaky door. It is dark inside. He opens the door a little bit more. He still can't see anything, there isn't enough light. He wants to turn and leave but he can't. He has to know if Ellen is there. As he flings the door wide open a slew of birds fly out the door, forcing him to duck. He walks inside and sees an old tractor, some bales of hay and lots of dust and cobwebs. Then he sees it, the source of the noise. As he turns to look over in the direction of the tractor it leaps down on top of him. He put his arms up to protect his face and falls back. It is a big, black-and-white furry sheep dog. He laughs as the dog is on top of him licking him!

"What's your name," laughs John. The dog just keeps licking him. He pushes the dog off to the side so he can get up. There is no one here; they obviously moved out. John feels a little bit of relief to think that no trouble will come from that day. Ellen is probably recovering fine and getting ready to start at her a school where she can forget Blytheville. She didn't live there for long but she probably doesn't have much she will want to remember, either. Either way John felt a tremendous sense of relief, still slightly curious but relieved. He walks out of the barn and the dog walks right beside him. He can't be a year old.

"So what am I going to call you?" asks John. "How about Buddy? You look like a good Buddy." The dog just jumps up on him again, which John takes as a positive response to the name. "Buddy it is then!"

They walk out of the farm and back through the woods. John plans to take Buddy home and introduce him to the family. He couldn't leave a puppy to starve. Maybe his parents will be happy to have an addition to the family since he and Jill will be leaving soon.

When John gets home he makes Buddy stay outside. He needs to introduce the idea of a new dog before he brings Buddy inside. He hears his Mom yelling for him, "John, is that you?"

He yells down, "Yeah Mom, I'll be right down."

He goes into the kitchen where his Mom, Stacey, is.

"What's up Mom?" he asks.

"Hi sweetie. How was your day?" she asks.

"Good. I was walking home and I was thinking, with Jill and I heading off to college and just you in the house, I thought you might get kind of lonely during the day. I thought you might want someone to spend time with," John says.

"What are you talking about John? What do you mean, someone to spend time with?" she asks.

"Let me show you. Now close your eyes Mom," John says, smiling.

His mom hears some scuffling and noise as John goes outside to get whatever it is. She hears the door open and more noise. She thinks, "What does he have?"

"Okay Mom, open your eyes," John says.

Stacey opens her eyes and can't believe it. "Oh my, he is a beautiful dog. Where did you get him? And more importantly, why did you bring him here?"

"His name is Buddy and I found him! Can you believe it? I had to bring him home with me, he's only a puppy," John says.

"John, I don't really need another thing to take care of right now. I hadn't really thought about getting a dog." She looks over at the dog,

"Well come here Buddy, let me look at you," she says. "Oh, you are a pretty one, aren't you?"

"I'm glad you like him, Mom. You think Dad and Jill will like him too"

"Honey, we have to discuss this. You can't just bring a dog home and expect that we'll keep him. I'll talk to your father when he gets home."

Jill gets home from school and is delighted with the new family member.

"Can I take him outside and play with him, Mom?" she pleads.

"Okay, but if you hear your father's car you need to bring him in!"

"Okay, promise. Come on Buddy. Let's go outside and play catch!"

They are playing for a while an hour before John's dad arrives home. When John's father, George, gets home, Stacey meets him at the door. She wants to break the news to him before he sees it for himself.

"Hey honey, how was your day?" Stacey throws her arms around George.

"Good," he replies curiously. "What happened, did someone get into trouble today?"

"No, why would you say that?"

"Oh, I don't know. You greet me at the door like I'm Ward Cleaver and I get a little suspicious."

"OK, I guess you're right." Stacey laughs and starts to walk into the kitchen. George follows.

"You know John and Jill are going off to college this fall." She pauses.

"Yeah, they're going to college, so?" He sits down at the kitchen table as she starts to set the table.

"Well, I was thinking maybe we could get a dog or something. You know, to fill the hole."

"Hole, what hole? Dog's dig holes, Stacey, not fill them."

"You know what I mean, George."

"Yeah, I do, and you know how I feel about dogs."

"I know but you're never home, it's usually just me, and I like having John here. When he's not here a dog would make me feel safer.

"Safer, from what?"

"I don't know George but just safer. I can't explain it."

"Well, we can discuss it in the fall. They're not leaving for a few more months. Why don't we let them graduate first, okay?"

John and Jill can't keep Buddy quiet for any longer. He lets out a playful yelp.

"What the hell was that?" George demands.

"Don't get angry, George. John found a dog today and he brought it home."

"What? Well it's not staying, Stacey."

"George, come on. What harm could it be for just a few days? Let's see how it goes. If it doesn't work out we'll take him to a shelter."

"You know, this is crap Stacey, right. You know that. The dog's here, the kids I'm sure are playing with him, and now I have to be the bad guy. You're putting me in a corner," he says, very frustrated.

"George," she walks over to him and puts her hands on his shoulders, "you know that wasn't the intention. What was I supposed to do when John brought him home? He was so happy."

George just puts his head down and shakes it side to side. "A couple of days, Stacey. If that dog pees in this house once, he's gone."

"Thanks honey," she says as she leans down to kiss him on the cheek.

That night Buddy sleeps in John's room. John lies in bed staring out the window. It is a windy night and he wonders where in the hell Ellen is. He remembers he found her backpack. He'll look through it tomorrow. John sleeps for the first time since the "event."

In the morning his mom has breakfast ready when he wakes up. He is starving. He sits next to Jill and eats his breakfast, passing pieces of unwanted food to Buddy.

"Mom, we need to get Buddy some food today," John says.

"I know we do, honey."

"Well, I can stay home from school today and help pick up everything Buddy needs."

"Nice try, John. No thank you, though. You're going to school and I will take care of getting everything that Buddy needs."

"You can't blame me for trying."

"No I can't. Now finish your breakfast or you'll be late for school."

"I can't believe we finally get a dog when I'm getting ready to leave," Jill says. "Oh Buddy, come here. I'm going to have to come home to see you! I'll take a picture of you with me to college so I can see you every day, too." Buddy just wags his tail happily.

John heads off to school after telling Buddy goodbye. When he gets to school he sees Mike and Cyrus out front talking so he goes up to see what is going on. He really wants to tell them about his visit to the house and Buddy. But he knows he shouldn't say anything. It'll just piss them off.

John walks up to Cyrus and Mike. "Hey, what's up?"

"Not much, man. Where were you yesterday," Mike asks?

"Nowhere. I just went home after school."

"No you didn't. I called your house," says Cyrus.

"I took the long way home."

"Long way," asks Mike? "What's the long way?"

"I walked by her house, okay?" He whispers looking around to see if anyone is watching.

"What the hell are you thinking John," snips Cyrus.

"Nothing, Cyrus. I just wanted to see if they were there. They aren't. I went out there and no one was there. They packed up their clothes, left all the furniture and moved out," John says. "Don't you think that's strange?"

"Right on, problem solved," says Mike smiling. He's half in the conversation; too busy checking out the girls.

"Well, whatever, man. I'm just trying to forget that whole thing. I'm glad they're gone," Cyrus says.

Mike and Cyrus turn to walk into school with John following behind them. Cyrus is whispering something to Mike and Mike is nodding. John knows they are talking about him and what they are going to do to him.

They get back together at lunch in the cafeteria. They are all walking through the line to get their food. Today it is green beans, mashed potatoes and meatloaf day, or at least it looks like that is what is on the menu. The cooks who work in the cafeteria look like they should be working a food line in a shelter. They are all overweight, with pasty skin, all in need of a quality facial. They wear hairnets, which only add to their appeal. As each student walks by they slop food on their trays, looking at them like their only happiness would be poison the food.

Mike never eats the food; he made friends with the women behind the counter and they always have something special for him. There are no limits to what he will do to get special treatment. Today it is a cheeseburger with fries. John is first to pay and then Mike and Cyrus. They take their trays of food and start walking to their table.

As they are walking to their table a brown-haired freshman girl comes walking their way. She's in old baggy jeans and a white slightly stained cotton shirt. She isn't looking directly at them so they can't tell who it is but she bumps into Cyrus. He drops his tray and his food hits the floor, splattering on his shoes and pants.

"Bitch," Cyrus screams! "Watch where you're going freak!"

"Sorry," she says and briefly looks up to make eye contact with Mike, and then quickly walks off, looking down at the ground.

"What is that all about," asks Mike. "She really messed you up, man. Look at that, you've got food all over your shoes!"

"Yeah, well why don't you go tell that little girlfriend of yours to hook me up with a cheeseburger and fries, too?" snips Cyrus. "I mean, it is bullshit you don't have to eat this food every day."

"Hey, calm down, man," says Mike. "Let me see what I can do."

They go sit down. Mike joins them a few minutes later with a cheeseburger and fries for Cyrus. Everything is okay, everyone is happy!

As they are sitting at the table eating they overhear some of the teachers talking about Ellen. She hasn't been in class for the last few days and no one has called in to say why. Mr. Delray is telling the other teachers that the principal tried to call their house and the phone was disconnected. No one has any idea what happened. He goes on to tell the other teachers that the principal has alerted the police so they can help find out what happened.

When Mike and Cyrus hear this, they immediately leave their food and get up from the table and leave the cafeteria. This is just what they need, the police to be involved. Now Mike is getting worried. Any trouble now will certainly be the end of his potential football career.

Mike's dad is friends with Judge Milford, so when Mike gets home from school he asks his Dad to find out what is going on. He tells his dad he heard some girl disappeared, he doesn't know her but everyone is talking about it. His dad says he will check into it.

The next day when Mike gets home from practice his dad, Bob, tells him what he found out.

"So I talked to John Milford today," Bob says.

"Yeah, what did he say?" Mike asks nervously.

"He says the police went out to the house, checked around and then called some of the folks who know the girl's father. It seems he just packed everything up and left. No one's living at the farm anymore. He had been struggling since his wife died, trying to raise the children alone, and I guess he just couldn't manage anymore. John assumes he took the kids and went back to Tennessee, to his wife's family, but he can't know for sure. Butch Dunn did get a call from someone asking if he wanted to buy any of his equipment. It looks like they're gone."

"That's it; did he say anything about Ellen?"

"No, that is it. I'm surprised the principal doesn't know."

"Yeah, that is weird. Thanks for finding out, Dad."

"No problem. Did you know the girl, Ellen?"

"No, no. I never talked to her," Mike says quickly looking at the ground.

"All right then, you hungry? I think Mom's got dinner ready."

"Yeah, starved!

# Chapter 3

Sarah Gregory has lived in Blytheville since she was born. She is a small girl with dark brown hair, often dressing like a boy, wearing hand-me-downs from her brothers. Her family has lived in Arkansas for two generations, originally immigrating from Italy and other parts of Europe. She grew up pretty sheltered, with two older brothers, Jacob and Jerry. Jacob is the taller and more athletic of the two while Jerry is more scholastic.

In sixth grade Sarah began watching her brother Jacob play football for Blytheville High. It was very exciting to watch the boys run up and down the field, hitting each other and running up and down the field with the football. That's when she noticed Mike Chambers; that's when the obsession began.

"Sarah," yelled Jacob. "Let's go."

"Okay, I'm coming." She yelled back. "Give me a minute. I still need to get dressed."

She kissed the picture in her hand and placed it back on the wall, in its proper place in the collage of Mike Chambers. She had been collecting newspaper clippings and photos of Mike for three years, all organized intricately on the wall in her closet. They were well hidden behind the poster of Italy her grandfather had given her for her seventh birthday.

"Sarah!" Jacob tried again. "We're going to be late for school."

"All right, all right." She threw on the jeans she wore every day and a t-shirt and headed downstairs.

"What were you doing up there?"

"Getting ready."

"Getting ready. You're wearing the same thing you wear every day. How long could that possibly take?"

"Stop complaining. Let's go."

# Chapter 4

The next several weeks seem to fly by. It is graduation day. What can be better? This is the time to celebrate the past and to prepare for the future. It is going to be warm today, 85 degrees and 90 percent humidity, so it is going to feel like 100 degrees. The football field is set up. The bleachers are trimmed with yellow and green ribbon, with big banners at the base of the announcer's box that read;

*Good Luck Class of 1998!*

The families are pouring onto the field, all dressed in their best Sunday dress. All of the little girls are tied up in ribbons and bows and the boys are in slacks and collar shirts. It is the event of the summer. Every family has their cameras out, ready to snap hundreds of photos of the graduates. This is a happy day and everyone is smiling with delight.

Today is the senior's day and everyone knows it. A yellow and green skirted stage has been erected in the middle of the field. There is an announcer's stand and microphone in the center of the field, with two rows of chairs on either side for the key speakers. The football field has been recently mowed so you can smell the fresh cut grass. The students' chairs are lined in rows, two equal sections, on the track in front of the stage. Everything is in its place, except the students.

All around there are kids primping, flirting and talking joyously about what the summer will bring. There is an announcement over the speaker system. The vice principal is asking the graduates to report to the gymnasium.

There they will go over the graduation program one final time. The vice principal is a nice man in his 50s with a soft spoken way about him. Most people call him Vice Principal Johnson but Cyrus likes to refer to him as Mr. Shiny. This is because of his receding hairline, which has virtually disappeared from the top of his head. It's always shiny. No matter what names he is called, Vice Principal Johnson is generally liked and respected by the students. If you look at their other option, Principal Williams, Vice Principal Johnson is an excellent leader.

"Today is a very important day," he starts off saying to the students. "It's not just an important day for you but for your families. That's why it's crucial that everything go well today. This is a time to show us all how respectful you can be and to set a good example for the younger kids, who admire you. There will be several speakers during the ceremony so speaking will be extremely rude. And we know that our graduating class has such nice manners." Laughter sweeps through the room. "As you walk out to the field you will walk in a nice single file line just like we practiced yesterday. Feel free to wave at your families but do not stop for photos. It will disrupt the flow. We ask that you please take your seats in a timely fashion and respect those around you. After the speeches have ended, Principal Williams will begin calling all of your names in alphabetical order, which is why you're sitting where you are. Upon entering the stage, I will hand you your diploma. It is at this time, you may turn to the audience for a photo. Please, please refrain from any obnoxious display of body bearing or name calling, etc. Once your diploma is in your hand, you are to walk off the stage and back to your seat, where you are to be seated. You will sit quietly until the last person is called and returns to their seat. At that time the principal will introduce your entire class and congratulate you on your accomplishment. This is generally when the craziness commences...you can throw your caps and have a little bit of fun. Thank you Class of '98. It has been a pleasure to be in your company. Now if you will, your principal." He motions to Principal Williams.

Principal Williams chimes in, "No pranks! Don't embarrass yourselves, your family, or the school!"

Vice Principal Johnson quickly says, "Thank you Principal Williams!"

Cyrus cracks, "Yes, thank you Principal Williams! Now shut-up!"

Principal Williams quickly replies, "Who said that? Tell me right now!"

But the crowd is silent. "That's the exact behavior I'm talking about. If we see any of it you will be removed from the field. No diploma!" His face is completely red and spit is flying from his lips as he speaks.

Mike makes his way over to Cyrus and says, "Are you high, man?"

"Yeah, I ran into this chick at the 7-11 last night and she asked me if I wanted to buy some stuff she found. The shit is killer. man. Why dude? Who cares?"

"I'm just saying man, keep up the comments and you won't get your diploma today!"

Cyrus laughs and says, "Who needs it anyway? I don't need a diploma to work at the plant."

Mike says, "Not me man—full ride to Michigan State my friend. College girls, here I come!" He smiles a smile that makes even Cyrus uncomfortable.

John joined in, "I don't plan on working at the plant, diploma or not. I'm getting out of here as soon as I can. I got accepted to Fordham in New York and I leave in three days."

"No way man, congratulations! It's sure gonna be hard without you guys around here," says Cyrus.

"Well, you don't have to stay; you can leave, too. They have financial aid," adds Mike.

Cyrus just turns and starts to put his cap and gown on. He knows he isn't getting out of Blytheville and he doesn't care. His sister is going to need him; she sure can't depend on his mom. The first John that offers to take her out of here and she will be gone. They don't have anyone else. He has to stay around.

John joins Mike and Cyrus and they put on their gowns. They know there is nothing they can do to convince Cyrus that he should leave. He is going to grow old and die in Blytheville. That is his destiny.

John is fussing with his zipper and Mike is talking with his best wide receiver, Ed, when Cyrus yells, "What the hell! Shit, I think I'm gonna throw up!" He falls to the ground clutching his side.

John hurries over to him and bends down, "What's the matter Cyrus, what's wrong? Do you feel sick?" He has no idea what is happening, he just figures Cyrus is nervous or took too many drugs and feeling sick.

This is a big day; it isn't going to get bigger than this for Cyrus. Graduating from high school is the greatest accomplishment he can hope for; no one in his family has graduated before.

Cyrus pants, "My side!" He curls over again and shrieks in pain.

John looks down and doesn't see anything. "You must be nervous, man. Let me get Vice Principal Johnson."

"Don't leave me man, don't leave me. Dude this is serious. I'm really hurtin', man."

Mike is talking to Susan when he notices the commotion and goes to see what is wrong. "What's going on? What's wrong with Cyrus?"

John looks up, "He says his side hurts. Go get Principal Williams, quick."

Cyrus shrieks again with pain.

Principal Williams comes back with Mike. "What's going on Cyrus, you don't feel well?" Cyrus is on the ground, curled up into a ball.

Principal Williams leans down and feels Cyrus's head. "We need to get you to a hospital, you're burning up. I'm going to call for an ambulance. You boys get his robe and shirt off to help cool him down."

He turns to see if there is someone else close by. "Cheryl, get over here. Go into the girls' room and wet some paper towels with cold water and bring them back, quick!" he orders and off he goes for the ambulance.

Mike and John quickly get Cyrus's robe and shirt off. Just as they finish Cheryl comes over with the cold towels and starts to put them on Cyrus's head and chest.

"What's wrong with him?" she asks.

"We don't know. He says his side hurts," says John. As John finishes his sentence he looks up and sees Vice Principal Johnson walking back toward them. At this point all the graduates are gathered around watching Cyrus and asking questions.

"Okay, the ambulance is on its way; let's get him closer to the door. You okay, Cyrus? We're going to have to move you. Everybody...on three. One, two, three." They all lift him off the ground and Cyrus's scream echoes through the gym. The entire room is filled with stares and chatter. People are talking, some gloating, some concerned.

Graduation is starting in 20 minutes. By the time they get to the front door the ambulance is pulling in with the sirens blaring. There are parents and students all around to see what all the commotion is about. Out of the school walk Principal Williams, John and Mike with Cyrus in tow. They are greeted by two paramedics with a stretcher. The paramedics take over from there.

They carefully place Cyrus on the stretcher. Cyrus screams out in pain. The paramedics check his vitals and question him about his pain. What has he eaten, drank, did he take anything, etc. The second paramedic questions John and Mike. At this point John is in tears from fear. What is happening to Cyrus?

"So who knows what happened?" he asks.

"Nothing, he just says his side hurt and then fell to the ground, curled up and started to sweat," says John.

"He didn't say anything else. Did he take any drugs? No one hit him, he didn't fall, nothing?" he asks.

"No, that is it. What's wrong with him?" John asks.

"It can be appendicitis. We won't know until we get him back to the hospital," he says and walks off.

They load Cyrus in the ambulance and drive off, sirens blaring.

Mike turns to John, "One of us should find his family and let them know."

John replies, "His mom's not here man, she never comes to anything. I'll see if Vice Principal Johnson can have someone call her at work."

The boys walk toward the football field as the ambulance sped off. The guys just wave. "See ya, Cy," says Mike.

"Yeah, later, dude. We'll collect your diploma for ya, man. You just hang tight," John adds.

# Chapter 5

Mike's parents, Bob and Susan, are so excited to see their son graduate, cheering him on as he walks the stage. They are one of the more successful families in Blytheville. His father started his own accounting firm when he graduated from college and it now offers financial services as well. They travel often, which allows Susan a glimpse into global fashion. She shops for them both. Mike's father is tall and slim. He is aging very well, very handsome. His hair is salt and pepper but cut short, which helps minimize the appearance of the gray. Clothes wear very well on his frame, especially Hugo Boss.

Susan is tall and slender as well. When she was younger she was considered to have a 'boy' frame. As she gets older she looks better in her frame. Her brown hair is colored to keep the gray from showing. She has faint blonde streaks flowing through that you can only see in the light of day. She visits her dermatologist regularly to keep the appearance of wrinkles to a minimum. She is 43, an attractive woman for her age.

As the boys collect their diplomas, they give a non-enthusiastic wave to their parents. After the ceremony all the kids are on the field with their families—it's photo time.

"Mike, Mike!" Susan yells to get Mike's attention as she's walking towards him, waving.

"Hey Mom, Dad." Mike gives them a hug.

"Congratulations son." Bob says.

"Thanks dad." A gloomy Mike replies.

"What's wrong son? This is a big day for you."

"I know. It's just that something happened to Cyrus before graduation. He collapsed on the ground with stomach pain and they took him to the hospital. I hope he's okay."

"Oh my goodness Mike, I'm so sorry." Susan states. "We can go to the hospital if you want."

"That would be great, Mom." Mike smiles like a sad little five-year-old boy.

They take some family photos and photos with friends.

"Hey Mike, one picture man, okay?" Ed says as he pulls Michael Gregory over for the photo as well.

"All right, but then I have to head out to the hospital."

"Okay, no problem. I hope Cyrus is okay, man. I've known him since we were kids too, man." Ed replies. "Hey Sarah, take a picture for us will you?" He asks Michael's sister.

"Okay, Ed." Sarah says as she smiles a devious little smile. "Smile pretty, Mike." She says.

"Dude, your sister is weird," Mike says to Michael. He just looks at her like she's a weird little freshman. They have no idea the plans she has for this photo. After the photo shoot Mike finds John and they get a ride to the hospital with their parents.

The boys run to the ER desk asking where their friend is. They are so frantic the woman at the desk can hardly understand who they are asking to see.

"Okay, calm down. Now who are you looking for?" The ER attendant says.

"Our friend, his name is Cyrus Flint."

"Okay, okay. Hang on a minute. Let me check the system. Is one of you a family member?" She asks.

"No, we're his best friends. We are with him when he keeled over," says Mike.

"Well I can't give out information on a patient to anyone but his family," she replies.

"What? That's ludicrous," says Mike.

"Yeah" agrees John.

"Sorry, them's the rules. You're welcome to take a seat and wait for a family member to arrive." The admitting desk clerk motions to the chairs in the ER waiting area.

"Dang," says Mike.

"We've got to get to his mom," says John.

They can't get his mom by telephone but they know where she works. They leave the ER and head over to the "Lounge." When they get there Cyrus's mom is just about to head on stage. They walk up to her to tell her what is going on but she isn't interested.

"Look," she says. "I'm about to go on. You're gonna have to wait."

Mary goes on stage and dances for 10 minutes. When she finishes the boys are waiting for her by the dressing room.

"Ms. Flint, look, we need to talk to you about Cyrus," John says. Mike is distracted, checking out all of the women who are walking around in thongs and bikini tops. They are wearing platform stilettos and strutting around like cats. Mike can't concentrate. He says hello to each woman as she struts by and gives her a Cheshire cat smile.

"What's he done now?" Ms. Flint snaps back.

"He's in the hospital; they don't know what's wrong with him. You need to come with us to the hospital."

"I'm working; I can't afford to miss my time on stage."

"Look, I'll give you 100 bucks but you need to come to the hospital with us now."

"One hundred dollars. Show me the money."

"Are you kidding me?" John cannot believe this woman. He pulls $60 out of his pocket. It isn't enough so he hit Mike. "Mike, Mike, pay attention. I need $40, man."

"Hey John, looking for a lap dance?" Mike hits John on the shoulder and gives him a look of approval.

"Mike, get serious. I need to give Ms. Flint some money so she'll come to the hospital."

"Oh yeah, man, I'm sorry. Here, take it." Mike hands John $40.

John hands the money to Mary.

"All right, well, let me get changed." She saunters off to what must be the most disgusting dressing room you could imagine.

Mary changes but the outfit she's wearing is almost as bad as the one she changed out of. She's wearing white Lycra pants that appear to be painted on with a low-cut pink sequined halter top and clear top stilettos. John's mouth drops when he sees her but he knew better than to ask her to change.

She goes with the boys to the ER. When they get there they see their parents in the waiting area but head to the nurse's desk first. Susan sees them run past. She has seen Mary before but each time it's like the first time...an unbelievable experience.

"Hi, any news on Cyrus Flint?" John says.

"I told you boys before. I can only release that information to a family member."

Mary leans on the counter, "I'm his mother, okay? Mary Flint."

The admitting clerk takes one look at her and asks for ID. She wouldn't put it past the boys to go out and find someone to play Cy's mom. She clearly looks like a woman for hire.

"Here, it's me. I'm his mom." She snips as she pulls out her driver's license and shows it to the clerk. She knows what the clerk is thinking and it pisses her off. "Good enough for you? I said I'm his mother. Now where is he?"

"Okay, well he's undergoing some tests right now," the nurse replies without looking up.

"Tests," Mike says. "What kind of tests."

The nurse turns to Mary, "They are running blood and urine tests to check for disease, metabolic disorders or toxins. Once they've finished they'll take a magnetic resonance image to look for bleeding in the brain, tumors, and infection. He'll have an Electroencephalogram, which will graph his brain output to help identify a metabolic imbalance. If none of those help determine the problem the doctor will perform a spinal tap to look for signs of meningitis and encephalitis."

"Lady," Mary says, "I have no idea what all that shit is, and don't expect me to pay for it."

"It's the tests that are going to help the doctors' figure out what's wrong with your son."

"Well, how long is this going to take?" Mike asks.

"It can take a while so you should all go wait in the waiting area," the nurse says as she points to the waiting area.

Their parents are standing behind them, trying to understand what's going on. They all walk to the waiting room. John's sister wants to go home so the fathers agree to leave while the mothers wait with the boys. They will call when they hear anything. They all leave and Mike and John and their moms sit down and wait.

They sit there for 20 minutes when Mike sees a girl walk by who looks oddly familiar. She quickly glances over at all of them in the waiting room. Her brown hair is up in a pony tail. She's wearing baggy jeans and dark blue tank top. Mike can't figure out who she is but he knows he's seen her before. On impulse he gets up from his chair and walks after her.

"Hey, hey you." He yells down the hall.

She starts to walk faster.

"Hey, wait up." He yells again as she runs through the doorway leading to the stairs. Mike follows her but she's quick.

"Hey, I just want to talk to you. Wait up." He says as he leaps two to three steps at a time.

She exits the stairway and runs through the lobby and out the front door. Mike tries to keep up but she's just too far ahead. When he gets out the front door he looks but he can't see her.

As he heads back into the hospital and up to the surgical waiting room he is bothered by the girl's identity. He's certain he has seen her. As he walks into the waiting room, John jumps up.

"Where'd you go man?"

"I thought I knew that girl but I couldn't catch up with her. I can't remember where I've seen her but I know I've seen her."

"So what man, you know lots of girls."

"No, I know. That's the thing. This isn't a girl I remember hooking up with. It's not like that. It's…it's…someone from school. I think it's that girl that bumped into Cy in the cafeteria…you remember, right? She almost looks like Sarah, Gregory's little sister, but I don't think it's her."

John stares at him blankly.

"It's been a long day." Mike sighs. "I don't know what I'm doing."

"Yes it has." John replies and pats him on the shoulder.

"Any news yet?"

"No."

They both sit back down for more than an hour before the nurse comes with news.

"I have some news. They have run all the tests. His internal organs are fine so he shouldn't need surgery. But he's slipped into a coma. They believe it's some sort of poison attacking his system. If that's the case he will be treated for a poison-induced coma. They'll give him a series of medications to counteract the depressive effects of whatever is causing the coma. It may work, it may not. They won't know for a couple more hours so you might want to go home and rest for a bit. It's your graduation today. I know he's your best friend but go home and spend some time with your families. We'll let you know as soon as we find anything out," she says and off she goes.

Mike quickly shouts, "Hey, nurse. Can we see him?"

"No, not right now."

John and Mike look at each other. What is going on? A coma from poison. Where did he get that? John's mother says, "Come on John. You heard the nurse. Let's go home. You can get something to eat and we'll come back as soon as they call."

"Okay Mom. Hey Mike, call me if you hear anything, okay?" John says.

"Yeah John, I will. You do the same."

"I will Mike. Happy graduation! I'll give you a call in a couple of hours"

They hug and leave with their moms to go home and spend some time celebrating what should be a happy day. They expected trouble during the parties after graduation; one of them would certainly get drunk and maybe end up in the hospital. But before graduation even starts, they never considered this.

When the phone rang Mike ran to the kitchen. His mom answers the phone so all he can do is watch her acknowledge everything she is hearing on the other end of the line. When she hangs up she looks like she has received bad news.

Mike asks, "What Mom, what did they say?"

"They said that Cyrus must have ingested something early today or yesterday that has sent his system into overload. His system it trying to fight whatever it is and in the process is shutting down. They need to get in front of it and they can't seem to. I'm so sorry Mike, but Cyrus is still in a coma and it doesn't look good!" She walks over to hug Mike but he just stands there.

"I can't believe it!" Mike says as he sits down. Cyrus was fine this morning, his normal self. "He is going to be fine, he has to be fine," he thinks.

He picks up the phone to call John. "Hey John, did you...you heard? Yeah, yeah man, I'll meet you there."

John turns to his Mom, "Mike and I are going to go see him. I'll be home later." John turns, grabs the keys and walks out. His family is sitting in the family room enjoying the day. They just watch as he walks out.

Mike and John arrive at the hospital at about the same time. Blytheville isn't very big. John walks in as Mike is asking the nurse what room Cyrus is in.

"You need to go down the hall and take a right; it's the third door on the left. Number 207," she says.

"Thanks." Mike turns around and sees John. "Hey man, he's in 207." John turns and starts walking with Mike to Room 207.

When they open the door they both stand still. Cyrus is lying in the bed with a tube in his mouth connected to a ventilator, which is making a noise they never thought they would hear. He has an IV in his arm that leads to two bags hanging from a rack, one is saline and the other is an antibiotic. There are machines everywhere and Cyrus seems to be connected to them all. He looks pale and cold.

Mike is the first to walk through the door, slowly. John follows. They walk closer to the bed. They have never seen anyone sick before, let alone hooked up to all these machines. Mike edges up to the bed and leans in and pokes Cyrus. He jumps back. Cyrus seems dead. John just stands in the background looking on. He thinks back to Ellen and what she looked like lying on the ground, lifeless and cold.

"Wow," Mike says. "It's like he's dead but he's still warm."

"Yeah, it's weird. Right?" says John. "Cyrus, wake up man! Come on, today's graduation," John says.

"You missed it man," Mike says. "Principal Williams almost fell when he got up to present the diplomas. Everyone laughed. Too bad he didn't fall, that would have really been funny."

"It was pretty funny Cyrus," John adds.

Cyrus doesn't respond. He is in a deep coma and the doctors have no idea what is causing it. John and Mike stay for about an hour when the nurse comes and tells them they needs to leave. They don't feel like joining any of the graduation festivities so they both leave and go to the bar just outside of town, Duke's. They just want to sit and have a beer together, try to let this all sink in.

Duke's is dead, not much going on, but it's the only bar within 50 miles. Everyone is at graduation parties. When they walk in they go straight to the bar. Dukes' is a small bar with six or seven tables, an old, oak wood bar with nine bar stools. The bar stools are weathered, they've seen many bar fights. Behind the bar are mirrors with shelves for the cheap alcohol they stock. The shelves haven't been cleaned in a few years. The cash register is an antique, gray, with each number having its own button. On the side is the handle that you pull to ring the sale into the register. It probably doesn't get used much anyway. Sitting in the middle of the bar is the tip jar; an old plastic pitcher that has seen more cheap beer than one would care to know about. They have Coors Light on draft and everything else is in the bottle.

There are pool tables on the right with ripped green velvet and a small dance floor. Just in back of the dance floor is the platform for the band. Behind the platform are old, red velvet curtains, hanging on just three hooks. No one is playing tonight, just the juke box.

"Hey boys, aren't youse graduating or somethin' today?" the bartender asks. "Today, you can have a beer on me," as he hands them a couple of Coors Lights.

"Thanks Donny. Yeah, we graduated. but without Cyrus" Mike says.

"What's that mean?" Don asks.

"Cyrus collapsed at graduation. They took him to the hospital but they can't do anything for him. He's in a coma now and they have no idea what's wrong with him." Mike says.

"No shit man, really." Don says.

"Yeah. It's fucked up man." Mike says.

"I'm sorry boys. That sucks." Don says.

After 15 minutes or so of silence Mike starts to look around the bar. There's an old man hunched over his Jim Beam at the end of the bar. He looks unshaven and hard, real hard. He must be a regular because the guy doesn't even have to order a drink. Don just fills it when it's empty.

"Here you go, Ed. You might want to slow down after this one." Mike overhears Don say.

"I'll tell you when I'm finished." Ed mumbles.

"All right Ed, all right." Don says as he walks back down toward the other end of the bar.

"Hey Don, who's the drunk at the end of the bar?" Mike asks.

"That guy, his name is Joe. He started coming here a few weeks back. He just sits at the end of the bar drinking every night. Doesn't say much."

"What a life." John replies. And just then, Joe turns his head and looks directly at the boys. His stare is hard, blank of any emotion other than pain and anger. Mike and John are surprised and don't know how to respond. They can't break his stare. Why is he staring like that? Don notices the boys in this frozen gaze and breaks the silence.

"Joe, you need something?" Don yells down the bar.

"No, nothin'." He grunts.

"What the hell was that about?" John asks.

"I don't know. He's obviously got problems. Just ignore him." Don says.

Mike continues to look around the bar and notices a girl at the juke box in the mirror behind the bar. Sarah notices he sees her, and gives him a little smile. After 10 seconds of staring at him she gets nervous and quickly looks down at the juke box. She's new at this, flirting. She's dreamed of the moment they actually talk but with the reality so close by she gets scared.

"Hey, take a look at the girl at the juke box," Mike says to John.

"You're unbelievable, man. We just got out of the hospital with Cyrus lying in a bed and all you can think about is a piece of tail," John says, then takes a drink of his beer.

"No man, that's the girl from school and the hospital," Mike says. She's changed her look again. Her hair is brushed and back away from her eyes, hanging down below her shoulders. She's wearing a jean mini skirt and a pink t-shirt with a flower decal on the front. Her shoes are black ballet slippers. Even with the different look, the eyes are the same. The same eyes that held his attention in the cafeteria and the same eyes he caught at the hospital.

"I don't really care, man," John says. "If you're gonna go after her then I'm gonna head out, man."

"No, John. I'm just saying she keeps showing up. I'm going to talk to her, find out why she's stalking me," and he take a drink of his beer and stares back at her.

"Leave her alone Mike! She's like 13 or something. She's a baby."

"Yeah, or maybe she's some crazy who's going to break into my house and steal my underwear and the hair from my brush. Make a voodoo doll." He laughs.

"I doubt it, Mike. But keep living in your 'Everyone wants Mike' world," John chuckles.

Mike smiles and looks back at the juke box. The girl is gone.

They spend the next hour talking about old times, all the things they did together growing up in Blytheville. All the trouble Cyrus gets them into. They laugh and reminisce until they're out of stories to share. Donny actually let them have a couple of beers. Just two, he knows they have to drive. They finish their second beer and then decide to head home. As they walk out Mike glances around to see if he can find the girl, but she must have left.

"Oh well," he thinks.

They get into their cars and drive off. John and Mike both plan to leave in a couple of days and have a lot to do to get ready. John just hopes Cyrus will wake up before he leaves. He can't stand the thought of not saying goodbye.

# Chapter 6

The bus pulls up to the Michigan football stadium and stops in front of the locker room entrance. One by one the Michigan State players walk off, grimaces on their faces. Mike is the second string quarterback, the golden boy waiting in the wings for the senior to graduate. He walks off the bus behind Ed, his best friend and roommate.

"Mike, hey, Mike." He hears from off to the left. He turns to see who's calling him. "Hey, Mike. What's going on man?" It's Jacob from high school. He hasn't changed at all.

"Jacob, what's going on, man?" Mike looks surprised.

"I walked on to Michigan. I'm red shirted but the coach might let me see some action today, when we run the score up on you guys." He laughs.

"Yeah, like that's gonna happen."

"So how you been, man?"

"Good, you know, getting used to Michigan. You know."

"Yeah. I know what you mean."

"Hey, whatever happened to that crazy sister of yours?"

"After that stunt she pulled, trying to hide in your car when you and Ed left for college, my parents sent her away for a little while, in New York near my uncle. You know, see if she can get some help."

"Hey man, I'm sorry about that. I just didn't know what to do, you know. I didn't expect to see her there. She scared the shit out of me. I almost crashed into the median."

"Yeah, well, I never understood why she was so obsessed with you anyway." Jacob let out a small laugh.

"Hey, it's good to see you, man. Hopefully I'll get to see you out on the field, right!" He gave him a friendly push.

"If you do, it will be running by you after I intercept your pass!"

They both laugh for a brief moment and then part ways to their opposing locker rooms.

# Chapter 7

College has been an interesting transition for Mike. Although he didn't play much his first year, Mike is still a huge part of the football team which makes his move into college very smooth. Paul Bennett, the current quarterback, is a huge help to Mike. He shows him the ropes with football, studies, the campus, you name it. After all...his successor has to shine and prove true leadership qualities if he is going to head up the team.

Mike has his fair share of conquests. Just because he is second string doesn't mean he can't pull chicks. The guys on the team always joke with Mike that he is in the wrong sport. He just laughs. But this year is the year for him to prove himself on the field and not just in the sack.

Mike's grades are mediocre; but he starts working with a freshman tutor named Sadie to help him stay afloat and on the team. She is unimpressive, to Mike. He sees her as someone who has no life except for school, a nerd. She is a small girl with dark brown hair she rarely grooms. Her face is round and pale, she hides herself behind big black-rimmed glasses. If you ask Mike what color her eyes are he will give a nervous laugh because he does not know. She wears unflattering clothes, intentionally. Sadie has no desire to attract attention to herself or her body, just living to her plan.

During the summer she goes home and works full time and tutors athletes during the school year. Michigan State isn't one of the schools that offered her a full ride so she pays 25 percent of her tuition. She started college with nearly a year of AP credits, all accomplished in her three years of high school, so she will be fine financially.

Mike has no choice but to work with Sadie once a week. Otherwise he will surely fail to keep up his grades and keep his starting position on the football team. Sadie is a thorn in his side, but she keeps him at a C average, which is just what he needs to stay on the field.

Sadie's roommate Cynthia is quite the opposite. She is very coordinated in her dress and concerned with her appearance. Cynthia is a very cute blonde from Chicago; she keeps her hair in a stylish blunt cut. Her personality is very dynamic and outgoing; her targets are usually young, cute and male. More effort is applied to deciding what she is going to wear than studying for an exam. She considers reading flipping through *Vogue*. Sadie and Cynthia couldn't be more opposite.

As they unpack, they start to get to know each other.

"So where are you from," Cynthia asks Sadie.

"Nowhere, really. I graduated from high school in Tennessee. How about you?"

"I'm from Chicago, born and bred. Never lived anywhere else, until now. I couldn't wait to get out of there. You know, controlling parent! How are yours—parents, that is?"

"My dad was okay, I mean as dads go I guess. My mom died when I was two so..."

"Oh, I'm sorry. That sucks. How did she die?"

"Does it matter?" Sadie whispers to herself, making no eye contract through much of the conversation. Friendships were not on her agenda.

"Hey, when we finish packing do you want to go get some coffee, check out the campus?"

"I don't know. I was planning on going through my schedule and getting ready for classes." Sadie continues to unpack her boxes and pulls out a jewelry box. She puts it on her desk next to a small potted azalea.

"Are you kidding me? No, we're going to check out the sights. You can get ready later. Oh yeah, and you know those flowers are poisonous, right?"

"Poisonous? Azaleas aren't poisonous. They sell them everywhere."

"Stick to law school, Sadie!" Cynthia laughs

For Mike, the first game of his sophomore year comes much faster than he imagines.

Mike turns to Ed, "It feels like school just started, man, I can't believe we're already suiting up for our first game."

"Yep, here we go, buddy. Second year and starting. It doesn't get better than this does it!" Ed smiles as he sees the coach walk up.

"Mike, this is going to be great! You're going to be great today!" The coach knows Mike will be nervous so he tries to help. "It's pre-season so let's just work the kinks out today, okay?" he says while he pats him on the back.

"Sure, Coach," Mike says. He puts his head down and continues his mental preparation. It is pre-season so some of the pressure is off. His parents have come up for the game; it is his big day. He really wants to play especially well for them.

The stadium is full as normal, with screaming college students and alumni. It is like a sea of green on a warm September day. The field is freshly mowed with pristine, white lines painted across and down the field. The Michigan State mascot is painted in the center, as always. The scoreboards are lit up and ready to track the progress of the game. The sidelines are prepared for the players with all of the necessary equipment and fuel the players will need through out the game. Everything is in its place.

The game passes quickly; at half time the score is 17–10, Michigan State. Mike is feeling pretty good about his play so far but knows he has to step it up in the second half. And he does. Michigan State wins the game 24–13! He goes to dinner with his parents to celebrate. After dinner his parents drop him off at the dorm. As they are walking across campus they run into Sadie. She doesn't even notice and Mike isn't going to point her out, but she literally runs into Mike's dad.

As she drops her books she says, "I'm so sorry!" She keeps her head down.

Mike's dad says, "That's okay sweetie, let me help you with those."

"Sadie, what are you doing out so late?" Mike asks.

Sadie looks like she's in her pajamas. She's wearing a pair of oversized blue sweats and a sweatshirt that's too big. Her hair is up in what must be a pony tail; it's hard to tell it's so messy.

"Oh, hi Mike. I was studying in the library and lost track of time."

"Mom, Dad, this is Sadie, my tutor." He mutters under his breath. "Sadie this is my mom, Susan, and my dad, Bob Chambers.

"It's nice to meet you Sadie," Susan says and holds out her hand. His Mom looks at her a little surprised. Sadie is young to be a sophomore in college. Sadie is still shuffling her books and doesn't want to drop them again.

"You shouldn't be walking around by yourself this late at night, young lady," Bob says.

"Mike sweetie, why don't you walk Sadie back to her dorm?" his mom says.

"She's probably fine, Mom," Mike says under his breath. He turns to her as if prompted and says, "Do you want me to walk you back, Sadie?"

Immediately Sadie snaps, "No, thank you. I'm fine," she says as she starts to walk off.

"Well, it was nice to meet you Sadie," says Susan but she just keeps walking. "Strange young girl, Mike. Why does she dress like that? I bet she's a pretty young girl under all of that, that, whatever she is wearing."

"Yeah, I don't think so, Mom."

"Where's she from?"

"I don't know Mom; we don't talk about that kind of stuff."

Off they walk to the dorm. They drop Mike off, congratulated him again and then head back to their hotel. They will drive home in the morning. Mike has a rendezvous planned for later...Lana.

Sadie gets back to her dorm room dumps her books on the desks and sits in her chair. Cynthia is laying on her bed reading.

"Hey, what's up with you?" Cynthia asks.

"Nothing, why?" She replies as she starts to organize her books.

"I don't know, you seem kind of flustered."

"I just ran into the Chambers."

"The Chambers. You mean Mike's parents."

"Yeah, they were walking him back to his dorm and I literally bumped into them. Of all people."

"Come on Sadie, what do you care? He's one of your students, that's all."

"I know, but his parents are so…so…I don't know the word I'm looking for."

"Uptight. Sugary sweet. Bland."

"No, it's nothing. I just can't believe I ran into them. That's all. What are you reading?"

"Ugh. It's my American History homework and it sucks. I mean, why does history have to be so boring?"

"Obviously you're not going to be a history major!"

"Nope," Cynthia laughs. "Wanna go get a cup of coffee or something."

"No. I'm kind of tired and I still have some homework to finish."

"Why is school so important to you Sadie, why are you in such a rush?"

"I don't know. I just want to go to law school, I guess."

"I get it, but you don't have to devote every minute to school to get into law school."

"I don't want to be in school until I'm 25. I want to get out and work, you know, make money."

"Make money. For your family?" Cynthia puts her book down and sits up on the bed. It's not often that she gets any insight into Sadie and her life.

"Yeah. I mean, my dad hasn't worked in years and my aunt still has my brother to support. He's a senior in high school. I would feel bad if I just partied and didn't work as hard as I could."

"I know what you mean. I'll be the first person in my family to graduate from college. Everyone is banking on me. I think that's why I party so much. Too much pressure."

"You'll do great Cyn. You shouldn't stress." Sadie smiles and turns back to her books. "I've got a couple of chapters to read. Maybe we can go out for coffee tomorrow?"

Cynthia smiles, "That would be great. Back to the history lesson. I should be asleep in 15 minutes!"

The East Coast is where John chose to start over. He is quite challenged to acclimate to New York City and Fordham University. The city is the polar opposite of Blytheville and he doesn't know anyone. He lives in the dorms with a roommate named Dan. They have become pretty good friends over the last year, dependent on each other as freshman.

Dan is from Oklahoma and came to New York to get away from the small town he grew up in. He and John have a lot in common. Dan is 6'3" with black hair and blue eyes; he is a handsome young man. Girls are very aware of Dan but he isn't too interested. He is always uncomfortable around girls, he just doesn't know what to say and it feels awkward.

John chooses to study political science and pre-law. He changes his appearance as he is getting much more comfortable in his own skin. He is growing his hair out, now to his shoulders, and it has a bit of wave to it. He dresses in much more fitted clothes, which are well coordinated. He is actually quite an attractive young man.

Even with all the city has to offer in terms of night life, John and Dan stay on campus most of the time. They venture out to hear a band occasionally but in general they stay on campus. There are always parties and events to go to; Fordham keeps the students pretty entertained. On the weekends they walk around the city—museums, restaurants, different neighborhoods. They both love the park and play Frisbee with their friends.

One cold, February night, John and Dan are out listening to Jam Machine at CBGB's.

"Man, I can't believe they can fit so many people into such a little space." Dan screams at John, who can hardly hear him.

"I know, it's insane."

"Let's get a drink"

"I'll have a beer, but only one. I have a big exam tomorrow."

"Yeah, yeah. I know. Gotta get into law school. Come on." Dan says as they walk toward the bar.

After three hours of body surfers, mosh pits and beer, Dan is pretty wasted. John isn't far behind him but still sober enough to carry Dan outside, which is no small chore. Dan is quite a bit taller than John.

The cab drops them off in front of their dorm room on the Upper East Side. It is a normal New York City block with everyone's trash piled up on the street. Next to their dorm building is the corner deli and a Laundromat. On the other side is an old Irish bar called O'Neil's. The bar brings a certain element in to the area that keeps things interesting. The building is an old pre-war seven-story building with fluorescent lights lining the hallways. The paint on the wall is a pale peach, which reminds everyone who enters of a bad grocery store. There is an elevator in the building but it is very old and slow. It creaks terribly as it goes up and down the floors. Most students take the stairs rather than risk the safety of the elevator. Dan and John's room is on the third floor.

"Come on Dan, help me out, man," he says as he pulls him out of the cab. Dan slurs something but doesn't help. John drags him into the dorm and to their room door. He leans him against the walk while he unlocks the door. By the time the door is open Dan has slid to the floor, laughing. He couldn't stand up on his own. He crawls into the room on his hands and knees, bumping into everything.

"Dan, you need to get into bed and sleep it off." Dan just slurs as he tries to reply to John. John lifts him up from behind, lifting under his arm pits. Dan falls into bed, taking John with him. John is pinned under the weight of Dan, who is now on top of him. They both stop for a second; John is getting an erection and he wonders if Dan notices.

"He's too drunk," John thinks. "What's wrong with me?"

Dan does notice and he doesn't mind. He is too drunk to think about why but he actually feels pleasure. A bit deadened, but pleasure. John is paralyzed by his erection and doesn't move. Dan looks at John for what seems like an eternity to John. He leans forward and kisses him. John doesn't move.

Dan looks down at John again; he is getting excited as well. He leans forward and kisses him again, and this time John responds. He kisses Dan back. John doesn't know if it is the alcohol or not but he is enjoying this experience more than he has enjoyed anything before. He thinks Dan is, too.

Before John knows it Dan is ripping his clothes off. Dan is still drunk and fumbles to get John's clothes off, so John helps. He reaches down and pulls his shirt off, Dan's as well. He can feel the heat of their bodies as their chests touch. Dan has a toned, cleanly shaped body with hard toned pecs that feel strong and firm, wonderful to John's touch. Dan's movements are rougher as he touches John's chest. He is hungry for John and is responding to his hunger. He pulls at John's pants; he wants to get him out of his clothes and to lie with their naked bodies touching.

It is all happening so fast. From the first kiss to John and Dan lying naked together, only six or seven minutes pass. Now they are lying together, exploring each other's bodies as they have never done before. Dan reaches down to feel John's butt and squeezes it as he pushes it into his penis. John screams out from the pain and the pleasure. Dan moves his hand around to the front and gently squeezes John's penis in his hand. He begins to stroke it hard and fast as they move together. Neither one of them knows what they are doing but it seems so natural. John begins to moan and move as Dan's hand continues to stroke his penis. He kisses Dan and pushes his hips back and forth, stroking Dan's penis. He is coming, he is exploding. Dan tilts his head back and moans loudly as John continues to move and firmly stroke his penis. He comes, hard and with a pleasure he never imagined.

Exhausted, they fall apart on to their backs on the floor where they pass out, lying naked next to each other. In the morning John is the first to wake up and he freaks when he sees Dan lying naked next to him. He jumps up and starts looking for his clothes. The noise wakes up Dan, who also is surprised to be lying on the ground naked with no one but John in the room. That night is the night that changes both of their lives forever.

# Chapter 8

John is ready to start his last year of school with Dan. He has adjusted to being who he is and has never felt happier. Mike, on the other hand...well, he has hopes of going pro but he isn't sure if it will happen. The NFL draft is around the corner and spots for quarterbacks are rare. This year will be his opportunity to solidify his reputation as a worthy candidate.

One more year of life as a student and then they will have to make their way. Both boys have been prepping for the "real world" their whole college life. They have fears just like the rest of the graduates. Will they succeed or fail?

Both Mike and John stop going home for the summer after their first year, spending their summers at school. After Cyrus got sick they were left feeling nothing but guilt. People expected them to go to the hospital and visit but it was really uncomfortable; it freaked them out to see him lying basically dead in a hospital. Sometimes it's just easier to avoid the entire situation. Regardless, Mike has football camp for most of the summer and John and Dan haven't yet shared their new relationship with their families. They don't believe they will be accepted back home.

John and Dan's relationship has become very serious; they are in love as deeply as two people can be. John continues his Political Science major and is still thinking about law school. And Dan finally chose his major, communications. He is so handsome and articulate that news anchor will be a most appropriate career for him. He figures the best place to try his luck at news will be New York. Lucky for him, he is already living there.

John has researched the local law schools; he doesn't want to get too far away from Dan. He knows NYU will be an excellent choice but not as easy to get into. Law school has a special meaning for John. He expects becoming a lawyer will ease his guilty conscious, giving him an opportunity to fight for the weak. He often thinks back to high school and wonders what ever happened to Ellen. The thoughts are too painful so he quickly pushes them down and replaces them with better thoughts of school and Dan.

They are excited for their senior year. They are happy together, doing well in school and have a good plan for the future. This is their last year and they are going to enjoy every day.

Back in Michigan, Mike is working hard to physically prepare for the football season. He has played starting quarterback for the past two years, taking his team to a bowl game each year. Several of his front linemen will be moving on to the pros and his lead receiver graduated. He is going to need to step up his game and depend on new, young players for team wins. As a fall back, and with the help of Sadie, he has chosen Finance as his major. His average has improved from a C to a low B, just enough to get into a good graduate school if football doesn't work out for him.

Michigan State is a beautiful campus in the fall, before the bad weather hits. The buildings are brick and very prestigious. The grounds are very well kept; the grass is always cut and the trees trimmed. The freshman dorms are some of the older buildings on campus. The brick looks old and weathered, with spots of white where the sprinkler system continues to hit the building instead of the lawn. As he walks up to the building there are parents and freshman students everywhere. It's like the Puerto Rican parade in New York City. There are young girls and boys with boxes, lamps, clothes, food, and mattresses being moved into the building. As parents finish unloading their young college student's things, the tears start to fall. Most of the tears are shed by the mothers but there are always a few young students who are scared of leaving home. Mike loves the start of each school year. Fresh meat! He's looking at a couple of young boys who obviously just met when he sees a cute little blond struggling with a box.

He thinks, "Well I have to go help her out, that box is bigger than she is."

He runs over to her right as the box is about to tumble out of her hot little arms, "Hey, let me help you with that," he says grabbing the box from her.

"Oh, thanks. It's really heavy."

"Yeah, it's about as big as you are. Don't you have anyone to help you with all this stuff?"

"No, my parents left because they didn't want to hit traffic."

"Well, let me help you with that. My name's Mike."

"Oh", says Sharon as she shyly looks to the ground not knowing what to say. Then she gives an awkward, "I'm Sharon. Nice to meet you. Thanks". They catch each others' eyes and he starts to move closer. Sharon clears her throat. "Thanks for the help. It's really nice of you."

"Anything for a new kid on the block," Mike says smiling. "Well, where am I taking this?"

"Oh, I'm sorry. It must be getting heavy just standing there with the box. I'm in Room 302."

"Oh great, stairs," Mike thinks to himself. "Great," he says. "I'll go ahead up."

"Okay. I'll just grab this other box and meet you upstairs," she says as she starts picking up the rest of her things.

Mike enters the small, green room. He looks around wondering where to set her things and just as he is about to drop to box, Sharon walks in.

"Oh no, not there." Mike is startled. He turns to her, box still in hand. In a harsh [[I don't think you mean strenuous]] voice, "Where would madam like her things?"

79

"I think this area is mine. How about here just on the bed."
Sharon motions to the bed and Mikes eyes perk up. They both giggle.

"Dirty minded, I see".

"Who, me? Nah. Well, thanks for the help, Mike."

Just then Sharon's roommate, Mary, walks in. She is struggling with a number of bags and boxes herself. Sharon opens the door for her. "Oh, here, let me help you".

"Oh my God, thanks" says Mary. "I am so exhausted."

"Tell me about it" Sharon concurs. "I'm Sharon."

"Hey, I'm Mary; nice to meet you."

"I hope you don't mind, I helped myself to this side..."

"Hey, not at all, first come, first served..."

"Well, I guess I'll let you two get to know each other." Mike says as he turns to walk out the door.

"Oh no, you just got here Mike. Do you want to go and have a coffee or dinner later? I'd like to thank you for helping me with my stuff," Sharon says.

"Sure, that sounds great. I'll stop by later," Mike says as he rushes out of the room. She seems a little too anxious, like a clinger. He is tired anyway from practice and wants to get back and study the playbook. Coach has added several new plays this year that he's expected to know.

The next morning Mike goes to the first practice of the season. The locker room is a dark, dark place, wall-to-wall gray. The floors are dirty and cracked, the sinks full of water stains and rusted faucets and the condensation from the molded showers give the room the incessant dismal smell of sweat. To Mike, this is home; he is back and glad to be back.

It is a cool day for a change, a light breeze is blowing. The field has just been cut for the first official practice of the season. Mike notices the "rookies" on the sidelines eagerly waiting for practice to start.

"How quickly that will change," Mike thinks.

Mike combs the field, taking it all in. He sees the cocky freshmen quarterback showing off his arm, throwing passes 60 yards downfield. Mike listens to the sounds of communal chants, the counting, the play calls, the coaches' screeches, the whistles, the birds. He takes in a deep breath to smell the clean air and the fresh cut grass. It is invigorating. Still in a daze, Mike's daydream is cut short by a ball to the chest.

He belts out a sigh, "It's....blah, blah blah," from the head coach. He rushes up to Mike, "Good to see my star back and right on time as usual". Mike high-fives the coach.

"Good to be back, Coach. You pack a hefty punch with that ball. Didn't realize an old man like you still had it in you."

Coach slaps him on his head. They walk toward the field. Everyone's eyes turn to Mike.

They warm up for about 20 minutes and then the real practice starts. Mike is in the groove, completing passes, scrambling out of the pocket and running the ball. He feels great! The only time Mike is a team player is on the field.

"Hey Ed, you gotta get an extra step on that play, man, or the defense is going to pick it off every time." Mike says as he pats Ed on the shoulder.

"Yeah, I know, man. I think I'm still slow from the summer off. I'll get it man, don't worry." Ed smiles.

"I know you will, man. You always do!" They give each other a high-five slap.

"What do you think of the newbie?" Ed asks as he gives a look to the young quarterback.

"You know, with some pre-season games under his belt I actually think he's gonna be pretty good." Mike says approvingly.

"I think you're right. I was throwing around with him earlier and he has an arm."

"Once he gets used to the pressure he'll do fine." Mike answers as the head back to the huddle.

After practice an exhausted and sore Mike walks back to his dorm. Right when the campus is coming to life for the rest of the students, his day is ending. He walks past groups of students just getting ready to head out for a night of fun. The campus is lush, green, and at this time of dusk, quiet. Mike takes the concrete path he has walked for three years. He looks around at all the buildings, reminiscing about what classes he took in each building. Some thoughts make him smile while others make him chuckle.

He nears his building and out from the bushes jumps a strange man, a homeless man. "Watch your back man…he is coming".

"Yeah, yeah, yeah" Mike retorts. "You have a good night, man." He looks behind him and the homeless man stands there staring. Mike laughs under his breath. "Man…they're everywhere". He keeps walking. A senior and he's still in a dorm. He will be glad when he's in a different living situation.

# Chapter 9

The first weeks of school are a blur for John and Dan as they settle into their schedules. They catch up with everyone about the summer and are fully engulfed in classes and studying. Dan has a part-time job at NY1 as a production assistant. It takes up quite a bit of his time, leaving little for John. But John doesn't mind too much since he, too, has a full-time job with school and studying for the bar exam that over 30 percent don't pass on the first try. The greater pressure comes from NYU, as they expect students to pass on the first try to keep up the school's greater than 95 percent average success rate.

Dan works on local news stories as well as generating story ideas related to life on campus. He is assigned a story on gay life while in college. A story Dan could write with his eyes closed and rightfully, a story Dan cannot wait to sink his teeth into.

"You seem so excited today babe, what's up?" John asks.

"NY1 asked me to do an expose on Jim Senda."

"Jim Senda, why does that name sound familiar?"

Dan's expressions are much more serious now. "Jim Senda was a student at Tulane University who was beaten by a group of male students when they found out that he was gay. It's not like homophobia is new, but Jim was an athlete. He showered with the guys, he worked out with the guys, and he acted like one of the guys. The pressure to come out was just too great so he hid it from everyone. But at some point he met someone that made him feel comfortable enough to risk it. They started seeing each other. The more they saw each other the more complicated it became. Jim was having a hard time hiding it so he broke it off. The boy retaliated by letting one of Jim's teammates know just who they were bonding with in the locker room. They were pretty brutal in taking out their anger on Jim. They beat him to death."

"Yeah, I remember that. What a horrible story? What exactly does the station want you to do for them?"

"Well, they want me to do a story, so I was thinking of picking 10 colleges across the country and asking them what being gay is like. I'd weave into the story how the campus reacted to the Jim Senda story and if it had an impact."

"That sounds great Dan. You can reach out to Pete, Tom, Roy, Steven—you know, all the guys we met during summer school from campuses around the country."

"That's exactly what I was thinking, honey." Dan walks over to John and puts his arms around his waist. "You are brilliant." And he gives him a little kiss.

"Well thank you, Reporter Dan." John kisses him back.

"I really do love you, John."

"I know sweetie, me too." And they hug.

Over the next few weeks Dan reaches out to several of their summer friends to get their views on being gay at their college. He takes the idea back to the NY1 and they love it. Each one of the interviewees remembers exactly what they were doing when they heard about Jim. They all have stories about how the story was received at their school. Dan puts together a short questionnaire designed to capture all the data and emails it to each participant. Then he begins the data-gathering process.

John focuses on his new role of campus president. He was secretary the previous three years and thinks this is the time. Winning the election will certainly help his law school applications. It takes up a bit of his time and gives him the opportunity to demonstrate his ability to lead in a political environment. He works on his draft agenda for the year, and makes several promises during the election; he plans on keeping his as first priority pioneering a better study area on campus. Most students go off campus because the school doesn't provide good study spaces. The second priority is getting increased funding for promoting the arts. After all, their school is in the middle of one of the most beautiful architectural cities in the world. The art world centers on its axis here…all the majors live and work in New York. He is thinking of a film symposium based on a Robert De Nero or maybe the photographer Annie Lebowitz. John creates a program that includes numerous field trips and on-campus lectures from curators, artists from all realms—fine art, sculpture, and performance art. After talking with some friends. he thinks inviting museum curators to come lecture at the school is another idea of interest. He has a lot of ideas; he just needs to focus his energy.

Sadie is just as driven as John, but is much more focused. If she keeps up her pace she will graduate early, top of her class in pre-law. She figures now is the time for a few changes. In the past, Cynthia tried to give her advice on how to change her look. Sadie is never sure what she will do with the advice but she listens to it. She and Cynthia have grown closer over the last two years.

Before school starts Sadie finally gets the nerve to make some changes. She goes into Vicky's Salon the week before school starts and lets them do their magic. They highlight her hair with lighter brown streaks and cut it around her face. The back is slightly layered to give the appearance of body and bounce. When they turn the chair around Sadie doesn't recognize her reflection. You can actually see her face now. She is still plain looking but now she looks groomed.

She buys herself a couple pair of jeans and some t-shirts over the summer and packs them for school. The jeans are much tighter than she is used to but they made her look hot. She just needs to get used to her new coiffed look. Sadie selects colors that Cynthia told her will work best for her; rust, turquoise, some stripes, etc. She arrives at school before Cynthia, unpacks her stuff, grooms herself, and put on her new clothes. Cynthia will arrive today and Sadie is excited to see her response.

Cynthia arrives with loads of bags and suitcases as usual. She rolls everything in; Sadie is looking in her closet as Cynthia walks in.

"Hi, what are you doing in my roommate's closet," she asks?

Sadie quickly turns around and watches Cynthia's mouth drop!

"Hi Cynthia. Did you enjoy your summer?

"Oh my God," Cynthia squeals. "I don't believe it. What have you done with yourself? You look fabulous!" She says as she drops everything and runs over to Sadie, jumping up and down. She runs her fingers through Sadie's hair, playing with her new hairstyle. Cynthia grabs Sadie's hands and pushes her back a foot so she can take a better look at her outfit, then spins her around to see the back view.

"Well, thank you," Sadie says as she turns red from embarrassment. "I took your advice and got my hair cut and bought some new clothes. It is our senior year and I can't exactly go to law school looking frumpy!"

"Well, you look great! I can't believe it. What did your aunt say? She must have died."

"She was surprised. She likes it, though. Not really the small town Tennessee look but she approved."

"Small town Tennessee. You're never going to see that town again!" Cynthia announced. "Let's go get some coffee and show you off."

They take their laptops and go to the local Starbucks just off campus. Coffee in hand, they sit to catch up and play each other in an Internet game of backgammon.

"So how was your summer? You're brother graduated, right?" Cynthia asks.

"Yeah, it was nice. My dad didn't show up but the rest of us were there."

"Bummer. He must have been disappointed."

"Yeah, but he's used to it. My dad started taking off when he was little so he spends most of his time with our cousin Tommy."

"What else did you do?"

"We went to New York City for the weekend with some of his classmates, on a graduation trip. My aunt and I went along as guardians. It was pretty cool."

"New York. Did you change your look before or after the trip?" Cynthia asked, leaning in towards Sadie and smiling.

"Before," Sadie said shyly with her head down.

"You go Sadie!" Cynthia squealed.

"How was your summer, what did you do?"

"Not much, I worked at my dad's gas station and hung out with some friends. Same as every year."

"Did you meet anyone new?"

"No, no one!" Cynthia sighed. "Unbelievable, you know."

"Yeah." Sadie responded but she had no idea what Cynthia was talking about.

Midway through their second game, Mike walks in with his parents.

Mike doesn't notice Sadie sitting with Cynthia.

"Hey Cynthia, you made it back for another year," Mike says, chuckling. He always flirtatiously toys with Cynthia as if she just might have a chance at getting a piece of him. But Cynthia has him dialed; she knows he is only talking to her to meet the girl sitting across from her. Mike doesn't recognize that it's Sadie sitting in that chair.

"Hi Mike, how is football camp?" Cynthia says.

"Great, you know. Another year at quarterback, it shouldn't be a problem to make it to a bowl again this year."

He might as well push his chest out and beat on it like a gorilla, Cynthia thinks to herself.

"Really, that's great Mike," Cynthia says completely uninterested in the conversation. Sadie is intentionally keeping her head down; she doesn't want to deal with the embarrassment of talking with Mike.

"Mike dear, what will you have," Susan asks. "A latte or mocha?"

"Latte, Mom." He screams across the room. "So aren't you going to introduce me to your friend?"

Cynthia laughs, "Are you kidding? Mike, its Sadie."

"Sadie," he bends down to put his face in her face. "Oh my God, is this the same, shy geeky Sadie that helped me get through the last three years! You change your hair or something."

"Well, I would say thank you but somehow I feel like I was just insulted," Sadie says barely looking up and making eye contact. "How was your summer?" She really doesn't want to know; she is just making small talk.

"Good, good. You look good, Sadie. Hey Mom, Dad, you remember Sadie, my tutor."

"Oh yes, yes, of course, how are you," Susan asks? "You look like you've changed your hair or something is different, yes? Whatever it is, you look just lovely."

Sadie is embarrassed by the compliments, or partially by the fact that she must have looked horrible before.

"Thank you. I just got it cut." Sadie is bright red at this point.

Susan continues, "Sadie, I just can't thank you enough for all the great work you've done with Mike, helping him keep his grade point average up. I just don't know what he would have done without you!"

"Thanks, but I can't take all the credit," Sadie says quietly.

Sadie just sat in silence, a very awkward pause of dead space.

Mike finally says, "Well I'll call you later, Sadie, so we can go through my course list. I'll need your help if I'm going to keep up my B average!" Mike gives Sadie a look that she doesn't understand.

"B average? Oh, okay Mike." Sadie finally catches on. He must tell his parents interesting stories about how good he is at his studies.

Mike walks out with his parents and gives a wave and a wink back to Sadie.

Cynthia is slightly stunned. "Can you believe that guy? How the hell do you tutor that ignorant retard?"

Sadie just shrugs her shoulders, "Let's keep playing." Sadie motions to the computers.

"Well, at least this is your last year with him."

"Yep, I should be graduating this year as well."

"What's your rush? I mean, you're not even 18 yet and you have enough credits to graduate in two years."

"I don't know, I just want to be finished I guess, get started with my life. We've had this conversation, Cyn."

"Why does life start after college? You're life is happening right now. Enjoy it."

"I know. I just have things I want to do."

"What things? Become a lawyer and work 100 hours a week." Cynthia chuckles.

"Yeah, but that's not all."

"Well, what is it? You should be dating and having fun. I mean, look at you now. You could get any guy on the campus."

Sadie's mood changed. "I don't want any guy, I don't want to date." She stated quite adamantly.

"I'm sorry; I guess I hit a nerve. What happened, your high school love break your heart?"

"No," she said sharply. "I didn't have a high school love."

"Okay, I'm just saying, most girls get their hearts broken in high school, you know. Guys can be real jerks when testosterone starts running through their veins."

"I've definitely seen that." Sadie said, and once the words were out she wished she could take them back.

"Yeah, what happened? Tell me."

"Nothing Cynthia, it was nothing. It wasn't me; it was my sis…my friend."

"Your sister?"

"No, it was a friend of mine. We grew up next door to each other so it was like we were sisters. Anyway, I don't want to talk about this, okay? Can we change the subject, please."

"Is this what your nightmares are about?" Cynthia asks.

"Nightmares, what do you mean nightmares?" Sadie's pulse is quickening. What is she doing in her sleep that Cynthia is watching? Why hasn't she mentioned this before?

"Nightmares, you have nightmares. You have since freshman year. I just didn't say anything because I figured you would talk to me about it when you were ready. I don't know what they're about. You just wake up screaming."

"I do, I didn't know." Sadie is trying to cover up as much as she can. "I'm sorry I'm waking you up at night."

"No, Sadie, come on. It's not like that. I'm just worried about you, that's all."

"Well, don't worry."

As Sadie finishes her sentence some of Cynthia's friends show up at the coffee shop and she realizes a perfect opportunity to make a quick exit. She gets back to her dorm and turns on the light as she walks through the door. Cynthia's stuff is still all over the place. Her bed is covered with boxes of clothes and shoes. Cynthia's closet is wide open with suitcases piled three feet high and falling out of the closet. She obviously had more important things to do than unpack. The wood floors creak as she walks across the floor to her side of the room to the answering machine flashing red.

The voice on the machine is Mike. Although Sadie would never admit it, there is something rather sexy and demure about the sound of Mike's voice. And when she hears it for the first time in months, she finds herself smiling girlishly. Silently she catches herself and shakes it off. She thinks about calling him back but she is tired and not in the mood. She waters her plants, they look a little thirsty, and kicks her shoes off, turns some music on and throws herself onto the couch, clicker in hand. She is grinning ear to ear.

Mike walks back from his afternoon practice. It's fall and the temperature has cooled down. The leaves are starting to fall from the trees as autumn approaches. This is Mike's favorite time of year because it reminds him of the start of the football season. He stops and talks with some friends. The buildings that house the older students are much nicer than the freshman dorms. The façades are tended to monthly by the same old maintenance man, Karl, who has been caretaker since anyone can remember. It's a miracle he's still alive but he is and every day he is greeted by thousands of students. He is the man that keeps this place beautiful. The brick is clean, no hard water spots, the lawn is well manicured, and all of the trees are trim and clean. And he has a tip-top crew that follows the strictest of rules to keep the interiors just as nice. When you enter the building the halls are lined with fluorescent lights but the tiles are nicer and more colorful. The doors to the building are nice mahogany wood with big brushed brass door handles.

Mike walks through the halls, and is greeted like a Windsor in Buckingham Palace. Everyone has high expectations for Mike bringing the school to a major victory.

"Victory" yells one student! Mike smirks and keeps walking.

"What's up, man" a student says to Mike. A slap of hands in the air and laughter is heard as Mike continues his path and another student high-fives him, "Kick some ass this year dude, major ass, you hear?"

"I'm gonna try" says Mike. He reaches his door, pulls out his keys, unlocks it and jumps inside, slamming the door behind him and sighing with relief that he doesn't have to deal with more kids praising him. He is nervous he will let everyone down but he has put up an arrogant guard that is both hard to miss and completely filled with insecurity. Mike tosses his keys onto the old desk that has probably had thousands of books and papers covering it for years.

He sees a flashing red light. He hits the button. As the messages play, he sits and takes his shoes and socks off and strips his shirt off his back. The first message is from his mom telling him that they have gotten off okay and will call when they get home. The next message is the young freshman quarterback asking if he can borrow the playbook tonight, he has misplaced his.

Mike thinks, "What a loser, how do you lose your playbook on the first day." The machine clicks as if it's finished. Mike looks disappointedly at the machine as if it's betrayed him. He is pissed that he still has not heard from Sadie.

She used to get excited when he called at the beginning of the year. He always assumes it's because she is secretly in love with him. She goes home every summer and he is certain her summers are always boring. That's when he realizes he doesn't even know where she's from or where she goes during the summer.

He thinks aloud, "Who does she think she is ignoring me like this". A big "pft" sound comes out of his mouth. Mike lies on his bed staring at the ceiling, where he used to have a picture of Giselle Bundchen. But tonight it is bare, just like his social calendar. It takes him hours to fall asleep but he finally does.

# Chapter 10

Sadie waits a week to call Mike back. When she does he is a bit upset but he moves past it. Mike expects a successful quarter, a grade point average of 3.0. He will have to work hard to bring it up above a 2.8. Sadie is much more comfortable with him this year and it helps. It makes the study sessions more enjoyable and Mike gets more out of them.

The football season has started off well, they are 2-0. Mike is upset about the second game; he was hurt early in the first quarter against Notre Dame. It's nothing. He'll be back in the next game, after he stays off his knee for a few days.

Mike and Sadie meet for their regular study session on Wednesday night. Tonight is different, though; Mike doesn't want to study. He wants to spend time with Sadie. He wants to get to know her, let her get to know him.

Mike's sitting at his desk in his sweats and a snug t-shirt that accentuates his body definition. His hair is wet from showering and he smells fresh and clean. The lights are all on, the room is bright. His books are open on the desk next to his laptop. He has a depressing look on his face when Sadie walks in.

"Hey Mike, everything okay?" Sadie says as she walks in and puts her stuff down on the brown couch next to the desk. She's in a pair of jeans and a really cute pale blue short sleeved V-neck sweater. Her hair is pulled back in a pony-tail.

"I'm really bummed, Sadie. We're doing well this year but I've already gotten hurt. But what would you care? You never come to the games anyway." He looks down at his lap.

"I'm sorry things aren't going as well as you would like Mike. But you guys will go to a big bowl game this year, right?"

"So you are paying attention," he smiles.

"Well, if you call reading all the flyers on the hallway walls paying attention, then yeah. I mean, they're kind of hard to miss!" She knows this is going to bother him but she is enjoying toying with him. She sits down on the end of the couch next to the desk.

"Well, it would be nice if you would come to at least one game before we graduate!" Mike puts his arms on his thighs and leans closer to Sadie. She can smell the scent from his shampoo.

"Cynthia did talk to me about going to watch you guys in the bowl game. I'm thinking about it. I just don't know if I'll have the time."

"Really," Mike says. When he realizes how enthusiastic he sounds he tones it down. "Whatever. I mean, if you make it you make it. It would just be nice for you to support the school and the guys you help, you know."

Sadie is getting great delight in watching him try to seduce her. She can't believe how obvious he is.

"Well, if I came to the game, it's not like I would see you anyway. You'll be playing the entire time. You won't even know I'm there." She says leaning closer to him. She is so close that he can smell her perfume and hear her breathe.

"I would look for you in the stands before the game." His voice is more of a whisper now as he leans even closer. Sadie can feel the heat from his body. "There's always a party after the game as well, you know."

"I've heard about the after parties. I think that's why Cynthia wants to go." Sadie giggles and tilts her head slightly towards her right shoulder. She is shamelessly flirting with Mike and he's eating it up.

"Well, it would be great to see you there, Sadie," he says as he reaches out his right hand to touch her arm. As he moves his arm from the desk towards Sadie one of the books falls to the floor and makes a loud bang. They both jump, startled by the sound.

"Well, we should probably start studying. I have another session right after this one." Sadie says as she moved back to grab her books.

Disappointed, Mike picks up the book and turns back to the desk. He needs a cold shower now!

The next morning Mike wakes up with a new focus. Winning games is the most important goal at the moment. A successful season and a Bowl win will clinch a good position in the draft. His grades are good and now he needs to just win games.

When Sadie wakes up she talks to Cynthia and tells her that if the football team goes to a bowl, and Cynthia still wants to drive down to the game, she'll go with her. It isn't for several weeks so she has plenty of time to get her studies in order.

"I can't believe it, you really want to go."

"Yeah, why not? I mean, I can't graduate from college and not go to a game, right?"

Cynthia jumps up and down, squealing like a teenager. "We are gonna have such a good time, Sadie!"

"I'm sure we will but we need to finish the season first. Now calm down and go get in the shower."

"Okay, okay, okay!" She sings. As she walks over to the bathroom her foot hits a small mouse lying on the floor. She screams!

"What the hell, Cynthia. What are you screaming about?"

"It's a dead mouse, look at it, a dead mouse. How the hell did that get into our room?"

Sadie walks over and picks it up by the tail and walks over to the window to open it up and throw it out.

"It's just a mouse Cynthia, calm down."

"That's disgusting. I'm going to complain. They need to spray for these things."

"Whatever you need to do, Cyn, just calm down and get in the shower. The mouse is gone."

"Ewwww." Cynthia says as she shakes her head. "You are way too comfortable with this stuff, Sadie," she says in disgust and walks to the bathroom.

The weeks do go by quickly and it's the end of December. The weather has gotten much colder, it's snowed twice. The beautiful green, lush campus is now brown and dry. The snow killed the last signs of life and now the students wake up every morning dreading the walk to their classes. It's cold and dreary. The semester has been long and challenging. Both Sadie and Cynthia are exhausted from studying. The idea of getting a few days away in Miami is exciting to them both.

Cynthia and Sadie rent a convertible red Mini and drive down to Miami. Cynthia books them hotel rooms at the Motel 6. They will hit the beach for a day or two before the game, go to the game, hit the beach again and then drive back.

It takes them a full day to drive down to Miami; they arrive at 10:00 p.m. on Thursday. They are tired and hungry so they find a diner. It's old and run down, with aluminum siding on the outside of what had to once been a trailer. The fluorescent lights are dim and flickering. They sit down in a booth with red faux leather that's ripped in numerous places. There's an old mini juke box on each table. For a nickel you can hear any crappy song on the menu. At this point they are slightly afraid to eat the food. They order food that's deep fried and cooked very well done!

"So Sadie, I can't help but wonder if your new interest in football has anything to do with Mike?" Cynthia smirks.

"Absolutely not. I just thought it was time to go to a game, like I said, I can't get through college without seeing a football game."

"Yeah, right."

"Oh come on, Cyn. What would I want with Mike?"

"I don't know. You do spend a lot of time with him and you don't have to."

"It's a job, Cyn."

"Sadie, you could tutor plenty of other students. You choose to tutor Mike. Admit it."

"No. I choose to tutor the football players and Mike happens to be one of them."

"Okay Sadie, whatever you say." Cynthia gave up. She could never win an argument with Sadie.

After dinner they check into a Motel 6. It's not much better than the diner. The room has dingy, stained yellow carpet with floral curtains straight out of the Brady Bunch. The bedspreads look like they bought extra curtains and threw them on the bed. They are poly bed spreads, 100 count mustard yellow sheets. The towels in the bathroom have been bleached so many times they're like rubbing sand paper against your skin. The room is damp and the place smells of mold. Sadie thinks of episodes of CSI, fearful if they had infrared glasses they would see the seed of a thousand men all over the walls and headboards. They don't sleep that night. Any tiny little tingle on the skin and they were swatting it as if to rid it of a fly or bug

The next morning Sadie and Cynthia get a quick cup of coffee at a local coffee shop. It certainly isn't Starbucks but it'll have to do since it's the only thing within miles of them. They suck down their coffee with a cringe and head to the beach. This is the first time Sadie has been in a swim suit since she was a child. She is a little nervous. The beach is covered with loads of people sitting under umbrellas on lounge chairs with bold colored towels. The sound of children screaming with laughter is faint against the crushing sound of the waves beating on the coast line. The water is a beautiful color of pale blue, so pale you can see the ocean floor.

The girls take off their shoes near the end of the boardwalk. Sadie steps her pale foot on the softest, whitest sand she has ever seen, natural pumice. It's almost to pretty to sit on! There are life guard stands every 400 feet with green and red flags indicating where you can and cannot swim. They pick a spot close to the water where they will feel the breeze of the ocean as it wanes and waxes. Nearby is a volleyball net with scantily clad bodies all sweaty as they jump up and down, spike, and dive. A ball aimed straight at Sadie closes in just north of the head. It startles her. But more startling is the handsome boy running towards her spewing apologies. "I'm so sorry, my bad" he said.

"Don't worry. No damage. I was just about to hit the water anyway" Sadie replied. She walks down to the water. The water is still pretty cold so she just splashes around a bit.

"The water's pretty cold, isn't it?" she hears from behind her.

She turns to see who is talking to her. A breeze blows her hair slightly as she turns her head to see who is addressing her. Her eyes meet the most crystal blue eyes. She gazes into them, completely speechless, and then takes in the rest of him: gorgeous, tanned body with washboard abs. He has sun bleached long, choppy hair and lips so full her mind drifts even further and she is standing there in a daze, pursing her lips as if she were dreaming. He's wearing red, black and white board shorts with a Red Hot Chili Peppers logo. His hair is long and fine, the wind easily blows it away from his face.

He smiles at her as she clumsily leans into him. She is speechless.

"Hi, I'm Scott. What's your name?" Sadie is completely red faced and doesn't know what to say.

"You could tell me what your name is; I'm not going to bite."

She laughs and looks down at the sand, moving it around with her foot, "Sadie. My name's Sadie."

"Nice to meet you Sadie."

"You from around here? Because I'm pretty certain I would remember seeing you." Scott snarls sexily.

Sadie giggles. "I'm from Michigan. We're down for the game."

"I should've known you weren't from around here. You seem different then most girls here," Scott says as he brushes the hair back away from her face. Sadie blushes and looks down at the sand.

"Oh yeah, it's a big game tomorrow. I go to Florida State so we're pretty excited about it."

"Yeah, we are, too." She's drawing circles in the sand and Scott slowly starts to move his hand through the sand to touch hers.

"I have a couple of boogie boards if you want to go out with me."

"Oh, I don't know how to do that," she says still looking down and playing with the sand.

"Don't worry. I'll show you. Let me go get them," he says as he runs to get them.

Sadie looks up as his back is toward her. What a gorgeous body, she thinks to herself. She looks over at her friends and Cynthia is looking right at her, smiling. She is mouthing something and Sadie knows it is probably vulgar. She turns to see Scott running back down towards her with the boards.

"Okay, let's go Sadie. Don't be nervous. The water's really nice and you'll get the hang of the boogie board. It's really easy and super fun," he says as he grabs her hand and leads her down to the water.

■■■■■■■■■■■■■■■■■■■■■■■■■■■■■■■■■■■■■■■■■■■■■■■■■■■■■■■■■■■■■

Her pulse is racing and the water is cold. They head out to the water and spend the next two hours playing student and teacher. She is having more fun than she ever has before. This is the first time she has been to Miami and the first time she has spent time with a boy that she isn't tutoring.

They tumble out of the water exhausted and laughing. They put their boards down on the beach and sit down. Scott lies next to Sadie, reaches to her face and brushes the hair out of her eyes as he gazes so intently it makes her melt.

"You were right. That was fun. Thanks for teaching me. I think I'm a pro now." They laugh together.

"No problem. You're a natural."

"How long are you here?"

"We're leaving on Monday."

"What are you doing tonight? There's a big pre-game party if you and your friends want to come."

"I'm not sure what we're doing but I can ask them," Sadie says just as Cynthia walks up with her magazines and all her belongings in her hand as if she's ready to go.

"Did I hear someone say party?" Cynthia says as she sits down next to Sadie. "Hi, I'm Cynthia."

She reaches her hand out to shake Scott's.

"Hi, Scott. Nice to meet you."

"Very nice to meet you, Scott." Cynthia eyes Sadie as if to give her approval on finding a hottie. "So what party?"

"I was telling Sadie about a big pre-game party we're going to tonight if you want to come. I have to warn you though; it's a Florida State party."

"That sounds great. We'd love to go," Cynthia says as Sadie shoots her a look.

"Great. It's at the Sig Ep house on campus. Call me later and I'll give you directions." Scott pulls out a pen and asks Cynthia for a piece of paper from her magazine. She rips off a corner and hands it to Scott. He writes his number and passes it to Sadie. As Sadie takes the paper, Scott holds her hand delaying a release.

"Okay, what time should we be there?" Sadie asks.

"Anytime after 8:00."

"Great. This will be fun. Thanks for the invitation. Now let's go eat. I'm starving!" Cynthia says.

They all get up and Sadie hands Scott the board. "Thanks again for the lesson, I really enjoyed it."

"No problem. I hope I'll see you later."

Cynthia butts in. "Oh, you will."

"Okay. See you later." Sadie says as the girls turn to walk away.

Cynthia nudges Sadie and says, "You bitch, he's gorgeous. Look at that ass!"

The girls turn around and see Scott running with his boogie board into the ocean.

"Cynthia! He was just teaching me how to boogie board, that's all."

"Yeah, that's all. He totally likes you. This is going to be more fun than I thought. I hope there are more like him at the party 'cuz girlfriend needs some Florida action."

They head back to the hotel after lunch, turn the radio on in the room and start to get ready. Cynthia brought the cooler of beer in from the car. They danced around, showered, drank beer and talked about who they hoped to meet at the party.

"Sadie's gonna get luckyyyy tonight!!" Cynthia sings.

"Stop it, Cyn."

"No way man, you're gonna get laid." She suddenly stops. "Shit, where did I put my condoms? You're going to need one…maybe two." She's shuffling through her cosmetic bag looking for a condom.

"I'm not going to need a condom Cynthia. I just met him."

"That's the best part!"

"I can't believe you; everything's about sex with you."

"Of course it is. I'm 20 years old, what else would I be thinking about!" She starts laughing and lies on the bed, pretending to have sex with an imaginary partner.

Sadie doesn't care. She's excited to see Scott!

When they get to the party at 10:00 the place is swarming with student bodies. They can hardly get into the frat house. The door to the

110

frat house is red and wide open. When you walk in all you see is a sea of people. The music is blasting and everyone is dancing and drinking. There are kids on the stairs, in the rooms to the right and to the left. They are pouring out of the house onto the front lawn, dancing and talking. They all look like they are having a great time. There are hundreds of people everywhere. There is a band playing; you can't see it but you can hear it. Everyone has a plastic cup of beer in their hand. Sadie thinks there will be no way they will find Scott but before they walk 100 feet into the house she hears Scott yelling, "Sadie."

He walks toward them and looks even better than he did on the beach. He has on a white cotton t-shirt that clings nicely to his body and dark blue jeans. His body is beautiful. His hair is hanging down around his face. He looks tan and freshly showered. She can't believe that her mind quickly starts moving to thoughts of lying naked with him. She blushes.

"Sadie, hi. I'm so glad you made it. Hi, Cynthia. Let's get you girls something to drink." He grabs Sadie's arm and Cynthia follows. Scott pushes people aside as they walk through the crowd. He says hi to several people as they walk past but he's not interested in talking to anyone but Sadie. Cynthia introduces herself to every guy Scott says hi to as she trails behind Sadie to the bar.

They walk up to a bar. It's a wood bar shaped like a horseshoe. There's a couple of fraternity brothers behind the bar serving everyone beer. People are lined up but Scott cuts right through the line. The bar is covered with beer. Scott asks her what she wants to drink. If she says nothing he will think she is a nerd but she doesn't know what beer will do to her.

"I don't know, a beer I guess," she yells. It is very loud inside.

"Okay." He grabs a beer and hands it to her. "Kind of loud in here. Let's go outside."

Sadie tells Cynthia she will be outside. Cynthia is fine. She's honed in on a hottie across the bar and makes her way to him.

"That sounds good." Sadie replies. Scott grabs her hand and they walk outside. To the left of the frat house is a group of trees. There are several people sitting in groups around the first tree drinking and laughing so they decide to walk to a few trees set farther back and sit down where you can still hear the music but at a much more enjoyable level.

"I'm glad you came. It's really nice to see you again. You look absolutely gorgeous."

"Yeah, we went out to dinner first."

"I'm glad you're here," he says as he takes a drink of his beer. Sadie is just holding hers.

"I really had a good time with you today, Sadie."

"Me too, Scott. I like boogie boarding."

"Yeah, it gets much easier the more you do it."

"I'll have to keep practicing," she says as she looks down to the ground.

Scott touches her face and pulls it gently toward him.

"Don't be shy. I'm really glad you're here with me… you don't need to be uncomfortable. I'm not going to hurt you," he says as he brushes her face with his hand. "I just want to get to know you before you leave."

Sadie smiles shyly and starts to look back down at the ground. Scott leans in to kiss her. He kisses her lightly on the lips. She doesn't move. She has never kissed a boy before and doesn't really know what to do. He leans into kiss her again but this time it is much longer. Sadie responds. She is feeling warm inside, a feeling she is unfamiliar with but she likes it. Scott holds her face in his hands and kisses her again; this time he uses his tongue. Sadie responds in a way that surprises her. She doesn't know how she knew what to do but she did.

Scott put one hand on the small of her back and the other on her hip. He tilts her back slowly until they are both lying on the ground. Sadie drops her beer off to the side. The warm feeling is now going through her entire body and she is completely absorbed in the feeling. Scott starts to kiss her again, soft, deep, passionate kisses that seem to never end. She doesn't want them to end, either.

"This is what I have been missing while I've been studying," she thinks to herself.

113

His hand starts to move up from her hip to her stomach and then right under her breast. She quivers from enjoyment. She doesn't want him to stop. He slowly moves his hand onto her breast and squeezes it gently. She moans with pleasure, pleasure she has never experienced before.

She can feel herself getting wet. She knows this feeling from her own exploration. Scott's erection is pressed hard against her inner thigh. It scares her and excites her at the same time. She arches her back into his chest as they continue to kiss. Scott's hand starts to move down from her breast back to her stomach. He can feel her quiver as his hand goes exploring. He moves further down to her belly button and then to the top of her panties. Sadie slides her foot up so her knee is in the air and then she lets it fall to the side as Scott's hand goes inside her panties. Sadie moves her hand down to Scott's jeans and unbuttons the top button. She slides her hand down inside his jeans. He is hard and a bit wet on the top. They are both moaning from the pleasure they feel. Sadie strokes Scott's penis as he moves his hips back and forth. As he moves towards her he thrust his fingers inside her. She is so hot and wet, it makes him more excited.

At that moment, the moment they are completely in a trance from the pleasure, a drunken guy comes tumbling over them. They both jump and sit up.

"Oh, I'm sorry, dude," the guy says as he stumbles back over to the side of the house and throws up.

"Sadie, I'm sorry. Maybe we should go to my room."

"No, that's okay. I should probably go find Cynthia."

"No, Sadie, stay out here with me, we don't have to do anything."

"I'm sure they're wondering where I am. I should probably go check."

"Okay, I'll go with you. I don't want you to go," Scott says as he touches her face lightly and kisses her gently on the lips.

"Okay." They both get up and go inside to find Cynthia. When they get inside they see Cynthia dancing on the bar. She has just finished her fifth beer bong and is feeling no pain.

"Oh no," Sadie says. "She's wasted. How am I going to get her back to the hotel?"

"Didn't you come with a couple other girls?"

"Yeah, but they didn't want to come here, they had another party to go to. They're supposed to meet up with us later."

"I'll help you get her back. Don't worry, Sadie."

"Thanks, Scott."

They get Cynthia back to the hotel. They have to stop a couple of times to let her get sick. When they get her into the room they throw her in bed, where she passes out.

"So do you want me to stay," Scott asks?

"You know, I'm kind of tired."

"Well, can I see you tomorrow?"

"I don't know. I'm not sure how Cynthia's going to feel."

"Well, I'll call you in the morning. I really want to see you." He leaned down, put her face in his hands and kissed her. There went that warm feeling again. She pulled away.

She needs to rush to Cynthia's side and deal with her drunken friend while she's saying her goodbye to Scott.

"Okay, call me tomorrow and I'll see how Cynthia feels," says Sadie.

"Okay. Night, Sadie. I'm really glad you came tonight."

"So am I. Good night, Scott."

In the morning it takes Cynthia a while to get motivated. She is hung over. All she wants to do is lie in bed and not move. Scott calls but Sadie tells him she needs to take care of Cynthia. He is disappointed but he understands. She tells him where she will be sitting at the game so he can come and find her.

# Chapter 11

Game day is hot and muggy. The team is leaving the hotel and heading to the field. Mike walks out to get onto the bus and as he walks outside he feels the heat and the humidity. It reminds him of Arkansas. Thinking of home always makes him feel sick. His mind starts to wonder back to Blytheville when the coach comes up behind him.

"Mike, you ready, kid? You don't look so good."

"No coach, I'm ready. Just thinking about the game."

"Good. This is going to be the game of your life, kid. Stay focused."

"Don't worry, coach. I'm focused."

He gets on the bus and sits down; he needs to keep his mind on the game. He starts to go through the plays in his mind, running through them like he is on the field. They arrive at the field and everyone looks around. They are the first people to arrive. It is eerie it is so empty. The stadium is huge compared to Michigan State. The building is much newer as well.

The building is made of white stone, and as you enter you see the huge sign *Federal Express Bowl*. The stadium is full of blue and orange bleachers, row after row. The stadium staff is getting ready for the game and you can smell the hot dogs and popcorn in the air. The stadium is clean, not a piece of trash to be seen. This makes Mike feel even more nervous. This is serious. It reminds him of the high school championship games, when all that matters is the football game. His mind turns to Sadie, he wonders if she will be there. Then he catches himself—why does he care if she comes? He starts to feel pinches of anger, which he's never experienced before.

They walk through the maroon-colored door to the locker room. All of the lockers are maroon, Florida State colors. There are benches lined in front of each of the bays of lockers. In the center of the locker room are a table and a white board. The coach requested the white board before the game. There are dirty white laundry baskets on the end of each aisle of lockers. Off to the left is a room with a door, which leads to a coach's office. In the back of the locker room is the whirlpool area. Mike is deep in thought, not talking with anyone.

They are expected on the field in 90 minutes. Mike is excited to get out and start throwing the ball around; he knows it will make him feel better, more confident.

Sadie and Cynthia hook up with a group of friends and get to the game about an hour before kickoff. They are all in jeans and Michigan State shirts. One of the girls has even painted her face green and white. Sadie thought that was a bit fanatic, but whatever. Sadie had bought a really cute short-sleeved green sweater for the game but decided to wear it after the game.

Cynthia is feeling better but not ready to drink again. It is a sold-out game, with green and maroon shirts everywhere. They are in their school colors and proud to be Michigan State students. The stadium is packed with mostly maroon shirts but there is a section hat looks like a sea of green. This is the visitors section, where Sadie is proud to be sitting. This is her first game so she's in awe of the noise, the people, and the atmosphere. It all seems so surreal. You can feel the energy in the air. The scoreboards are flashing the team names and the lineup. There are explosions and smoke. The teams come onto the field, and when Michigan State is announced the girls go crazy. The crowd screams "Go Spartans!!"

Both teams run into the middle of the field for the coin toss. Sadie notices Mike is one of the Spartans on the field; he looks good in his uniform. Spartans win the toss so they decide to kick off. Once the ball is in the air the game flies by quarter after quarter. Mike has an excellent first half; 21 of 26 pass completions and rushes for 50 yards. The Spartans are ahead by seven. Sadie and Cynthia head to the concessions stand and grab some food before the second half. Cynthia is looking a bit pale.

While waiting in line, Scott walks up, "Hey girls, I've been looking for you," he says as he grabs Sadie and gives her a kiss.

"Hi Scott, good game don't you think?" she says.

"Yeah, it's close but it's not over yet. Cynthia, you don't look so hot."

"I don't feel so hot either. I need some food and a Coke."

"So what are you guys doing after the game?" he asks, hoping to see Sadie again.

"I don't know. It depends on how Cynthia's feeling."

"I should be fine. I think some of our friends are having a celebration party after the game, assuming we win, of course."

"Well, then it looks like you guys are going to need something to do," Scott says, laughing.

"You think so, do you?" Sadie says, pinching him in his stomach.

"Ouch. Don't hurt me...yet anyway," he smiles and leans down to kiss her.

"Okay, well give me your cell number so I can call you after the game and we can meet up," Scott says.

"I don't have one, but Cynthia does. Do you mind?" she says giving Cynthia a look that says "Please give him the number!"

"Sure, it's (410)555-9816."

"Got it, I'll call you later; okay," he says, leaning to kiss her goodbye. She gave him a short kiss and says okay.

They get their food and head back to their seats. Mike throws the ball back and forth with his top receiver. It's odd, but in that instant Sadie swears Mike looks into the stands directly at her.

The second half goes almost as quickly as the first. Mike doesn't perform quite as well this half but his running backs made up for it. The Spartans win the game 41 to 30 and the crowd goes crazy. The fans rush the field in celebration and tear down the goal post. The fans are pretty drunk at this point so they are fumbling around the field, yelling and screaming. Some are screaming out of joy and some out of anger. Not a good mix. Cynthia and Sadie stay in the stands and watch. What a sight it is! This is only the beginning of the craziness that is to be their last night in Miami.

Sadie decides it will only be right to go to the Spartan parties; she is a Spartan, after all. The party with the players doesn't start for a couple of hours so they go to a bar nearby where some of their friends are meeting to celebrate. Cynthia is feeling much better now, ready to drink again. They line kamikaze shots up on the bar and everyone takes one, even Sadie. Then they hand beer out to everyone in the place!

"Go Spartans," someone yells and everyone drinks. The time flies by and before they know it everyone is heading over to Lowes for the party.

The ballroom is quite large and decorated for what would seem to be a wedding. There are green and white balloons everywhere. Every table has white linens with green linen on top. The centerpieces are Michigan State footballs stacked on top of each other and tied together with green and white ribbon. They have the date and victory game printed on the side. There are three bars strategically located around the room. Waiters and waitresses follow the drunken people around catching their glasses before they drop them. There are a couple of tables on either side of the room with a buffet of food.

There are hundreds of people, everyone wearing green and celebrating the victory. A guy with a microphone talks about the team's victory and asks all the players to come up to the stage. That's when Sadie sees Mike; he's changed into a t-shirt and jeans. He looks clean and refreshed; quite attractive. All the players look happy and ready to party. They worked hard for this victory and for many, this is their last season. Several will go on to play professionally but many will not; this is it. They are going to enjoy every minute.

"Let's get a drink, okay?" says Cynthia

"You're ready to go again, I guess." Sadie smiles.

"Of course," Cynthia smiles back and heads over to the bar. Cynthia's phone rings but she doesn't hear it. It's Scott trying to reach Sadie.

"Wasn't that a great game?" Tim asks Sadie. Tim is one of Cynthia's freshman year conquests. They slept together once and decided to just be friends.

"Yeah, it was exciting." Sadie replies.

"I can't believe it...does it get better than this?" Tim screams.

"I guess not," Sadie says, laughing at Tim. He's turning in circles, screaming. He obviously had too much to drink at the game.

"Here you go," Cynthia says as she hands Sadie a beer.

"Thanks."

"Cheers!" They tap beer bottles.

Several beers later everyone is pointing and laughing at the coach, who has decided to get up on the stage and dance. Someone grabs Sadie's hand and pulls her away. Before she knows it she is over in a corner with a large man pressing his body against hers.

He looks down at her, "I've been looking for you!" It is Mike.

He leans down and kisses her. Dazed from the alcohol, she wraps her arms around his waist for stability. They kiss for a few minutes and then Mike says, "Let's get out of here."

He grabs her hand again and pulls her out of the party and into the elevator. He hits a button and then pushes her into the corner and starts kissing again. It is all happening so fast she feels like she is on a roller coaster. Mike's very strong. The elevator stops. He grabs her hand again and pulls her down the hall to his room. He opens the door and quickly has her on the bed and is on top of her.

"Where are we?" Sadie slurs.

"In my room. That's okay, isn't it?"

"I guess." Sadie's slurring is getting worse.

He kisses her again, but this time he is much more delicate. She feels his erection on her thigh. Mike takes his top off, then hers, and undoes her pants. He moves his hand up to her breast, Sadie isn't wearing a bra and that excites Mike. He moves his mouth down her neck onto her breast and starts sucking her nipple. Sadie moans with pleasure and pain as he bites down firmly on the end. She reaches down inside his pants and grabs his penis. She can hear how much he enjoys it as she strokes him firmly. She pulls his pants off using her hands and feet. He rolls her on top of him and does the same with her pants. Their bodies are warm as they press against each other.

He kisses her the entire time, moving her closer to the top of the bed. Sadie is on top of him, stroking his penis with her vagina. He moans as she rubs up and down him. Each time she comes to the top, the head of his penis slips inside her, just a bit. He fumbles for a minute but then quickly picks her up by the hips and thrusts her down onto his penis with great force. Then Mike rolls her over so that he is on top of her. Her legs wrap around his waist, he pumps slowly in and out of her. He is slow and steady, watching her match him stroke for stroke. When he sees that she is ready he starts pumping faster and harder. Her moans get louder and faster; her legs squeeze him tighter. Within 60 seconds Mike has reached climax. He collapses on top of Sadie's sweaty body, and starts kissing her again.

"Oh my God, that was great," Mike says.

"Yeah. I don't feel so good." Sadie gets up and runs into the bathroom and starts throwing up.

"You okay, Sadie?"

"Yeah," she screams back from the bathroom. "I'm fine. I just don't feel too good." She really wanted to scream, "I can't believe I slept with you...you jerk!"

"Can't hold your liquor, Sadie!" Mike laughs.

# Chapter 12

The hospital is cold and sterile with the smell of bleach. The fluorescent lights are bearing down like the lights in an insane asylum. Cynthia screams in pain, wishing someone will make it stop. She feels like knives are piercing her sides and stomach without pause or hesitation. The pain is so severe that she begins to vomit. The nurses are trying to help but there is nothing they could do. They need the anesthesiologist but he is in surgery so Cynthia will have to wait. Each minute that passes the pain gets worse, and she screams louder.

The nurse screams down the hall, "If you don't get her someone now it's going to be too late!"

Another nurse yells back, "We're paging Dr. Rosenberg but we haven't heard back from him. We don't have anyone else."

"Well find someone NOW," she yells back. "She can't take much more."

As the nurse walks back into the room, Sadie is sitting next to the bed pressing a cold compress on Cynthia's head to try to calm her down.

"We're trying to find Dr. Rosenberg but he's not answering his page."

"I don't give a shit who's not answering a fucking page, do something NOW! Do you hear me, NOW?"

"I understand you're in pain but there's nothing I can do and yelling profanity at me won't help."

"How about if I strangle you? Will that help?" she screams as she thrust forward toward the nurse's neck.

"Cynthia, what are you doing?" Jerry screams. "Honey, you need to calm down."

"Jerry's right Cyn," Sadie adds. "Threatening the nurse isn't going to get a doctor here faster. Let me go see what I can do."

As Sadie walks out of the room Cynthia turns to Jerry, "Calm down, calm down. This is all your fault," she starts crying. "It hurts so bad. Please Jerry, make it stop."

"Honey, I wish I could do something for you, but I can't have the baby for you."

"No shit, Sherlock! I don't know why I married you, you're an idiot! You're an IDIOT," she screams as the contractions come like a tsunami. If she doesn't get her epidural soon she is going to miss her window and she knows it.

As she finishes screaming at Jerry, Dr. Rosenberg walks in with a nurse and Sadie following behind him. "I'm here, I'm here," he reaches down and gives Cynthia a peck on the cheek. "How are we doing sweetie? The pain's bad, I take it. Let's take a look." He checks to see how far along she is and looks up with a look of bad news. "I'm sorry sweetie, but you're already nine centimeters—this baby is coming without the drugs. Nurse, gives her something in her IV to ease the pain and let's get ready to bring this baby into the world, shall we?"

"You are kidding," Cynthia cries. "I can't do this without drugs; I told you that, I can't do it."

"Cynthia, honey, you can do it. Come on, just focus on what you learned in class," Jerry says holding her hand.

"I can't do it, Jerry," she cries. "I don't want to. It hurts."

"Come on Cynthia, let's get ready to push, sweetie," Dr. Rosenberg is pushing her legs apart and pulling her down to the end of the table.

"Stop calling me sweetie or my foot is going to go in your mouth."

"Cyn!" exclaims Sadie.

"Okay, the pain must be pretty bad. Let's get this baby out. Now push for me Cynthia, push hard."

Twenty-five minutes later Jerry and Cynthia welcome a beautiful baby girl they name Nell Grace Winters. She is 6 pounds 10 ounces and 21 inches long, perfect in every way. They wrap her in a hospital blanket and put a pink net hat on her head. When the nurse hands her to Cynthia, she cries. She looks up at Sadie and the tears start running down her cheek. Sadie feels nothing but smiles at Cynthia.

"She's beautiful Cyn! Really beautiful."

All the pain is gone and now Cynthia has this little beautiful person in her arms. The grandparents are patiently waiting in the hospital waiting room. Sadie is the only friend welcomed for the actual birth. Everyone else will have to wait until they bring the baby home.

"Jerry, isn't she perfect/" Cynthia says as she brushes Nell's cheek with her index finger. "We can call her Nellie Grace."

"She's perfect, honey," Jerry says with tears welling up in his eyes. He gives Cynthia a kiss on her forehead and then stares back down at Nell. What a day. You wake up in the morning and everything is one way, several hours later everything has changed.

The nurse comes in to move Cynthia to her room.

"We're going to take the baby and get her cleaned up and checked out. We'll bring her right back to you when your settled in your room, okay!"

"Okay," Cynthia says, exhausted.

"I'm going to head home Cyn, you need to get your rest." Sadie says as she reaches down to give Cynthia a kiss on her forehead.

"Thanks for being here, Sadie. I couldn't imagine having Nell without you here. You'll be next, right?"

Sadie's face goes pale, "Yeah, yeah, I'm next." She chuckles. The idea of having a baby makes Sadie nauseous. She turns to Jerry. "Do you need anything Jerry?"

"No, no Sadie, I'm good. My parents are here and they'll take care of everything at the house. You sure you don't want to stay at the house, too? There's more than enough room."

Sadie smiles a fake smile, "No, thanks Jerry. My place is just fine. I've got exams this week anyway, I need to study." Sadie is finishing up law school at Columbia. My dad's coming tomorrow so I'll stop by after I get him settled."

"Why don't you bring him with you? We would love to meet your dad."

Sadie, obviously uncomfortable with the idea, answers, "Thanks, Jerry. Really. But he doesn't really like hospitals." She looks down at Cynthia, "You get some rest."

"Bye Sadie," Cynthia says, half awake.

Two days later they take the baby home to her perfectly designed room. The families are at the house with several of their friends. Everyone is excited to see the baby.

Jerry and Cynthia's home is in Scarsdale, New York. The homes were built in the early 1900s but remain stylish and clean. Jerry and Cynthia chose their home not for size, but because of its curb appeal. The house was set back about 200 yards from the street with a giant oak tree in front. Hanging from the oak tree is a swing made of wood. The driveway is short enough that you can see the house from the street. The driveway is lined with mums of three different colors, red, orange and yellow.

The house is an English Tutor, all red brick with dark green ivy growing freely on the front. When you walk into the home the living room is off to the left and the master bedroom to the right. There are three smaller bedrooms and two baths on the top floor. In the back of the house, on the main floor, is a glassed-in solarium Jerry has turned into his relaxing room. It has caramel leather chairs, a ceiling fan and a 64" flat screen TV with surround sound. There's a glass door that takes you out to a stone patio.

On the second floor, Nell's room is painted the prettiest color pink with unicorns flying up to the moon above her mahogany wood crib. Her bedding is green twill with pink washed silk trim and a hand-sewn lace bed skirt. A mobile of elves hangs above her crib to help her sleep. There are mahogany shelves on the wall for all of her childhood treasures. All of the gifts they have received are sitting wrapped in the corner of Nell's room. Cynthia and Jerry wanted to wait until they had the baby to open up many of the gifts.

Jerry's parents have hung pink balloons all over the house to welcome Nell home.

Jerry and Cynthia married shortly after graduation in Michigan. This wasn't exactly how Cynthia saw her life playing out, 21 and marrying a 33-year-old investment banker in New York. Jerry works for JP Morgan in the financial district.

Jerry is the lead manager of the company's foreign investments division. He started his career right after graduate school at Columbia and never looked back. Since taking over this division two years ago, the division has achieved record profits for it investors and the bank. Jerry is being groomed for much greater roles.

# Chapter 13

The building on 3<sup>rd</sup> and Lexington is in a complete blaze of fire. Firemen from all over the city have come to help put it out. News crews and cameras are everywhere, trying to keep the city informed. Helicopters are buzzing around above, taking shots from the sky and trying to help the firemen determine how best to put out the fire. Everyone is fully engaged when a loud explosion shot out from the 5<sup>th</sup> floor. Glass goes everywhere and four firemen are blown from the building. Anyone within 10 feet of the building is now lying on the ground bleeding and half deaf from the noise. One helicopter is caught by debris and smoke is pouring from its engine. The pilot attempts to land on top of a building several hundred yards away from the fire.

As people run screaming and medics attend to the injured, Dan continues to cover the scene.

"It's unbelievable here, the building just exploded, injuring several people. We don't know how many but several people are lying on the ground bleeding. Medics are getting to as many as they can but this is a devastating sight," he says yelling over the noise around him. Dan is live at the scene and is being fed questions from the anchor covering the story on air in the newsroom.

"So Dan, tell us, do you know what caused the explosion?"

"No Brian, we don't know. It will take some time before we can find out; this is a crisis situation. The building is still ablaze and people are very hurt and sadly, some lie dead on the street. It's unbelievable."

"It certainly sounds like it, Dan. What an absolute devastation! All of our thoughts and prayers go out to the families affected by this catastrophe and we will be in continual communication with Dan so as to know what the latest reports are. Thank you, Dan. Hang in there and be safe."

"Thanks, Brian." Dan is off the air now, looking around to see if he can determine what is going on. It is a massive site of destruction, but he seems to be the only reporter still standing. This is his chance for a big break, an anchor job! He has to make sure he covers this with all the information an anchor will need. He has to be compelling.

He runs around the scene with his camera man asking questions and gathering data. As he gets information he feeds it back to the network so they can report it in the city. It is beautiful. He works it like a pro. When he gets home he is exhausted and excited. John is studying in the office with Vivaldi playing in the background. Dan grabs a bottle of wine and two glasses and heads into the office.

John is startled, "What the hell happened to you—are you okay?" He walks over to Dan to see if he is okay.

"Okay, I'm great." He gives John a hug and kiss and a gentle crotch grab. "Hi, hun. I am thoroughly exhausted."

John replies, "You look like you've been hit by a train."

"Haven't you heard what happened today? A building on 3$^{rd}$ and Lex caught on fire and then exploded. It was the most devastating event I've seen. But...I got the entire story!"

"Oh my God, I had no idea. I've been locked up in here. Studying all day; I haven't even turned on the television. I can't believe I'm finding good in this, but, I'm glad you got the story; that's great, honey."

"I need a drink in a big way. Part stress relief and part celebration. My first big story."

"Okay, but just one. I have to study. Finals start tomorrow and I need to focus."

"Okay honey, just one and then you can get back to your studies. I need to clean up and take a nap. I'm exhausted."

After their drink, Dan takes a shower and John returns to studying. He is in his last year of law school at NYU and is graduating in the top of his class. He doesn't want to screw it up now. He has already passed the bar so all he needs is a good end to his last year and he can pick which firm he wants to work for. He already has several firms interested in him so life is good.

He finishes studying at around 11:00 and goes into the bedroom. Dan is passed out in bed so John makes his best effort to be quiet while he undresses for bed.

In the morning John gets up and Dan is already gone but left a note for John on the bed.

"I have to get in to the office early today, expecting a lot of praise for yesterday. See you at dinner. Love you."

John reads the note and smiles. He is really proud of Dan. He gets ready for class. He stops to get coffee on his way to class, runs into a few friends, chats for a bit and then heads to campus to get settled before his exams. He has one exam at 9:00 another at 1:00 and yet another at 3:00. He will grab lunch in between.

He's tense and nervous about his exams. He rushes into the coffee shop and orders a latte with skim. He sees a couple of his friends at a table as he's walking to the sugar station.

"Hey Greg, what's going on?" John asks.

"Studying, how about you?"

"All night. Let me sweeten my coffee and I'll come sit with you guys for a minute."

John is rushing because he doesn't want to be late and bumps into a coffee patron at the sugar station.

"I'm sorry," he says. "It's that kind of day."

"I hear you. Here's a lid for your coffee…so you don't spill it," she replies, smiling.

"Good idea. Thanks." He puts the lid on and then goes and sits with his friends.

They are talking about their exams and how they feel they went.

John gets to his exam on time. The first four hours are grueling, but it goes well; he knows he aces it. He is pretty exhausted so he heads to the café to grab some food and refuel for the next exam. He sees Greg in the café so he decides to sit with him and talk about the exams. He forgets to buy a soda for class so he goes back to buy it and then returns to his seat and his friends. He finishes his sandwich and salad and pulls out a book to look over a few things before the next exam. His friends are doing the same thing, asking each other questions, when they notice John drop his book. They look over and John has fallen out of his chair.

As he falls out of his chair his drink crashes on the ground and spills all over the floor. The sound of his fall startles everyone sitting around their table. They all start to stare as John lies limp on the floor, eyes wide open. It's like he can see everything that is happening around him but he can't speak or move. People are standing over him and talking but he can't hear them. His heart is beating fast and his body is beginning to shake.

"Oh my God, John, are you okay?" one friend says as he gets up and runs over to John.

"John, what's wrong, John?" the other friend asks.

"Someone call an ambulance, quickly," the friend yells.

They try to help John but they don't know what to do. He can't speak; he just lies their gasping for air. He can't breathe.

A crowd starts to form when the campus emergency medical team arrives. You can hear the questions from the crowd, "What happened? Do you know who that guy is? Is he going to be okay?"

The medical team rushes up to John, push everyone back and immediately start to work on getting a ventilator into John so he can breathe. They put an IV in and lift him onto the gurney and wheel him to the ambulance. It happens in a matter of minutes. John's friends don't know how to get in touch with Dan so they leave a message at John's house.

Dan has a great day; he is the star of the network! He is right; he got offered a promotion on the weekend morning show for his great reporting. He is ecstatic and cannot wait to tell John. When he gets home John isn't there. Dan assumes the exams are running long or John stopped to talk with some friends. He sees the light flashing on the answering machine and walks over to play the messages as he pours himself a glass of wine.

The first message is from a friend congratulating him on his success. He chuckles and smiles as he listens to the message. The next message is a bit cluttered so he turns the volume up.

"Dan, Dan this is Greg....Greg Moran, a friend of John's from school. I'm not sure; I mean we don't know what happened. Something happened to John, the ambulance took him, and I'm not sure where—I think Mt. Sinai but we're not sure. I don't know what happened, he just collapsed. Anyway, this is the only number we have. Sorry."

Dan stops completely as he listens to the message, his mouth falls open and the glass drops from his hand. He presses play again in a panic to get the message right. He is not sure what he heard. As the message plays again, Dan falls to the floor holding his stomach. This perfect day has just turned into the worst day. He picks up the phone and immediately calls Mt. Sinai to see if John is there and he is. Dan grabs a cab and rushes to the emergency room.

Crazy thoughts are going through Dan's head while he's journeying to the hospital. His cab driver understands the urgency and is switching lanes at 40 miles an hour to try to get to the hospital. Dan is so dizzy and distraught that everything is blurry. All he sees are lights flashing by him. He starts to feel like he can't breathe. The cab quickly pulls up to the emergency room and slams on the breaks. Dan flies forward and hits the glass between him and the cab driver. The stop snaps him out of his trance and he pays the cab driver and jumps out of the car.

There's lots of activity in the emergency room. The waiting room is yellow with fluorescent lights. The chairs are hard and curved, like you would expect in an airport. The waiting room is full. As he approaches the nurse's station he is in a complete panic. There are three nurses sitting behind the desk working at the computer and looking over patient's charts. They don't even notice as he run up to the desk.

"I'm looking for John, John Gillman. He collapsed at NYU University a few hours ago."

"Okay, first you need to calm down," says one of the nurses. Her badge says Georgia but Dan doesn't notice. "Gillman, Gillman, and here it is. Are you a relative?"

"No, I'm not a relative; I'm his…his partner." Dan can't believe he doesn't know what to call his relation to John. "Where is he? I need to see him."

"Well, I'm sorry you can't. He's in ICU and only immediate family can see him. We've contacted his parents and they're on the way."

"What do you mean I can't see him? I have to see him, what's wrong with him?" Dan says sobbing. One of the other nurses comes from behind the nurse's stand and puts her arm around Dan to help calm him down.

"Okay, calm down. I'm sure you're very upset, but you really need to calm down, okay? Let me see the chart, Georgia," she says, giving Georgia a look of disgust. "Let's see what it says…" she turns the pages reading the notes. "It looks like he had a seizure but the cause is undetermined until we get the test results back. He's on a ventilator so he cannot talk to you anyway. I can walk you over to his room and you can take a look inside but I'm not supposed to do this.

"Thank you, thank you so much," Dan is still sobbing. "I just need to see him, you know," he says as they walk toward the room. "What kind of results are they waiting for; what tests did they do?"

"They're running several blood tests to try to determine the cause. If that doesn't work then they'll do a CAT scan and see if there's something going on inside his brain."

They walk to his room window. Dan stands outside John's room, looking in through the window. The room is painted white with tan curtains. There is a bed against the wall, a TV hanging from the ceiling and a door that leads to a bathroom. There is a picture cheaply framed and hanging on the wall. It's over an ocean scene. Dan sees John lying in a bed hooked up to a ventilator and what looks like 100 other machines. The room is not too large so all those machines make it look even smaller.

"Oh John," he says putting his face in his hands. Now he is crying. "John, what happened, John? Please tell me he's going to be okay, PLEASE!" It is no use; Dan breaks away and runs into the room.

"Stop, you can't go in there," the nurse says as she goes after him.

Dan runs up to the bed and put his face right next to John's. Crying he caresses his cheek and gives him a kiss. "Please. God; you have to pull him through this! John, you have to pull through this, I can't live without you."

The nurse pulls on Dan's arm and leads him out of the room. "I'm sorry; you're just going to have to wait for his family to arrive."

"But they don't know he's gay," Dan says crying. "I can't tell them. What am I supposed to say?"

"Oh, dear," the nurse says. "Why don't we figure that out when the time comes? For now, can I get you anything to make you more comfortable while you wait?"

Dan just has a blank stare.

She leads Dan back down to the nurse's station and gives him a cup of water and sits him down in the waiting area. "Just wait here. We'll let you know if we hear anything from the doctors or his parents."

Dan just shakes his head. He is in shock. The sight of John lying in that room is the most frightening thing he has ever seen. He has never given a thought to life without John but now that's all he can think about. Life is going so well for them both and now this…he doesn't even know what "this" is. With that realization the reporter in Dan kicks in. He starts to ask himself question after question. He wants to get up and runs out of the hospital but he has to wait to find out some news. As soon as the nurses give him more information he will go find John's friends that were with him when this happened. He needs to find out what happened.

Dan stays at the hospital through the night and into the next morning. The nurses tell him there is still no change so he decides to go home and get showered. On his way home he will stop by the school to see if he can find John's friends.

When he gets to the school no one is there. It is late and exams are over. He can't remember who left the message so he runs back to the house to play the message again. When he gets there he feels sick. What if John never comes back home again? Will he stay there, will he move? He pushes the thoughts out of his head and runs to the answering machine. He plays the messages. He can't believe he doesn't remember the name; he is a reporter, after all. He should remember these details. Greg Moran, that's it. He fumbles through the desk for John's address book. He keeps all of his school friends' numbers in it. When he finds it he quickly fumbles through the pages to the Ms. He finds the number, grabs the phone and dials. The phone rings but no answer. They are probably studying. He leaves a message giving Greg his cell phone number and asking him to call him as soon as he gets the message, whatever time.

He puts the phone down and looks around the house. He can't stay there; he has to go back to the hospital. That's when he starts to

144

think about John's parents. He has never met them. What is he going to tell them? What if they want to stay at his house? This is not the time for parents to find out their son is gay. He starts running through the apartment to hide anything that will reveal their secret. He runs upstairs to their bedroom and takes things from his room and throws them into the extra bedroom. He scatters his stuff around and then goes back into their room and cleans it up. The entire process takes him over an hour and he is exhausted. He sits down for a minute to rest.

Dan hears someone shuffling with the door knob and is startled. It sounds like they have keys but the wrong keys. Maybe they are at the wrong house. He gets up, dazed, he has no idea how long he has been sleeping. He looks at his watch and it is 2:00 a.m. He has been asleep for hours. He feels a vibration in his pocket. He pulls out his cell phone to see that he has missed two calls from Greg. When he starts to open the phone to dial Greg back he hears the front door open and some people talking. He looks around the room for a weapon and grabs a pair of scissors that are on the desk. He looks at the scissors and rolls his eyes. A lot of damage he can do with a pair of scissors. But it's all he can find. He starts to move towards the front door, approaching quietly so he can catch the intruder by surprise. He hugs the wall closely so the intruder can't see him. He's walking as quietly as he can but the apartment is old and the floor creaks. He stops quickly. When he determines the intruder hasn't heard him he continues to approach the door. He comes from behind the dining room wall and jumps out with the scissors raised high above his head. John's mom lets out a loud scream!

"Oh my God, I'm so sorry. I thought you are robbers or something," he says as he quickly put the scissors down.

"You must be Dan, John's roommate," John's dad says as he reaches his hand out.

"Yes, Dan, the roommate. I'm so sorry Mrs. Gillman. I didn't mean to scare you."

"That's okay Dan. It's been a long night and I need a drink and a bed."

"Any news on John, how's he doing?"

"The same," John's Dad says. "They have no idea what's wrong with him."

"Jill knew something was wrong with John, she called us earlier," John's Mom says. "Dan, will you mind getting me a drink. I could really use one."

The accident with John, no news on his progress and now hiding his relationship with the man he loves more than himself, it's just too much for Dan. He needs a drink!

"Sure thing Mrs. Gillman, what would you like?"

It is going to be a long night!

# Chapter 14

Dan travels to Blytheville with John's parents to bring John home so that they can care for him. It has been six months since John went into a coma. John's parents and his sister Jill came up as often as they could but it was time to move him home. The doctors didn't know the cause of his coma and it wasn't likely they would figure it out. And Dan's investigation came up empty. He questioned Greg shortly after the accident, just after John's parents arrived. But Greg had absolutely no information that was useful to Dan. No one did. It was like John just collapsed out of the blue, for no reason.

As they pull into the small town of Blytheville, Dan looks out the window to take it all in. It reminds him of home. Now he knows why John never wanted to come back. There's a local barber shop right next to the country store where everyone buys their goods on account. Dan thinks how amazing it is to still have towns in the United States that do not change. He rolls down the car window and takes a deep breath, trying to feel what John must have felt growing up in Blytheville. John's mother is telling Dan tidbits about each store they go by and who lives in each home. Dan just responds with a quiet, "Really?" He's not listening. It's obvious John's parents are very proud of their home town. Everyone waves at them as they drive by; they know the entire town!

As they stroll through the town Dan notices young boys playing football. John's mom tells him how it reminds her of John and his buddies in high school. She tells him about Mike, who's now a professional player, but they never see him. Then she tells the story of Cyrus, also in a coma.

This is when the investigative bells went off in his head. Is there a connection? It seemed odd that two boys from the same town fell into a coma for no apparent reason. They were really good friends growing up so they obviously spent a great deal of time together. Dan's head races with all sorts of ludicrous ideas; are there toxins in the water, or some pollutant that affects the people in the area? Did both boys come across some hazardous material that slowly grew inside them and eventually led to a coma? Maybe the school had asbestos leaking every day that they were in school!

As these ideas are consuming Dan's thoughts they pull up to John's house. Tears well up in Dan's eyes. This is where the man he loves grew up, the place that he went home to everyday. The house is nice, yellow brick with a white wood front door. There's a two-car attached garage. A basketball hoop is still up in the driveway. Giant elm trees shade the house and provide a very peaceful feeling to the home.

As they enter the front door a dog comes running up to John's parents.

"Down boy, down Buddy." John's Dad says. "Dan, we'll have to tell you the story of how we got Buddy later."

"I'll assume John's in that story somewhere!" Dan replied.

They continue in the house. John's mom offers to show Dan John's room, the room that he will be staying in while he's there. It's right next to Jill's room. Dan thanks her as he walks into the room. She says something to him and then closes the door behind her but he has no idea. He is consumed with thoughts of John.

The room must be just as John left it. It's painted a pale shade of blue. There are wood shelves on the wall with photos of John as a child. Dan picks them up and looks at each one for several minutes. He pictures the stories John told him in his mind as he looks at the images. There's a double bed in the center of the room with a blue comforter and a baseball blanket on the end. The nightstand has an alarm clock and a photo of John and his dad. Dan picks up the photo and sits on the end of the bed, continuing to look around the room. He starts to cry.

John's desk is clean, no papers, but there are two paperweights. One is from Disneyland and the other is of the Yankees. There's a small lamp on the right side. The wooden chair is old but it looks comfortable. Dan goes over to the closet and opens it up. It's clean, well organized. Some of John's clothes hanging on plastic hangers. The shelf above has shoe boxes, a couple of old speakers, a camera box and a black bag. Dan reaches up to grab the back and a couple of the items fall down and hit him in the head. His head softens the fall so not too much noise is made. He picks everything back up and puts it back on the shelf.

Dan lies back on the bed, still crying, holding the picture of John.

When Dan wakes up it is dark outside. He looks at the clock on the nightstand. He's been asleep for eight hours. It's 2:00 a.m. He gets up and puts the picture back on the nightstand. The twinges of pain come back. He can't sleep so he turns on the light and sits at John's desk. He opens the drawers and looks through the contents. Nothing too interesting. When he opens the drawer on the right he finds a photo of John and two other boys. He's never seen Cyrus but he has seen photos of Mike at work. His mind starts to race again.

There has to be a connection. He doesn't believe in coincidence. In the morning he plans to investigate the conditions in the area. If that doesn't get anywhere he'll have to track Mike down. He's the only one of the three that is untouched. He must have answers.

In the morning, after having breakfast with John's parents, Dan goes to the library and pulls up newspaper articles to get educated on the history of Blytheville. If there is something toxic in the community it will have affected more people than just Cyrus and John.

The library in the town is nothing like the public library in New York. It is a small brick building, circa 1979, and the layout is all on one floor. The front doors are white with glass windowpanes inserted in the door panels. There is one window on either side of the doors framed by white shutters. Above the door, written in gold letters is, "Public Library." When you walk in there is a desk to the left with a little old women standing behind it. She has that classic old woman, shaky hand syndrome with age spots all over. Her lipstick is a frosted peach color and drawn on well above her lip lines so as to appear that she still has full lips like she may have had as a young woman. She uses a black beaded chain with clips for her bifocals. Her silk floral blouse is right out of the '50s.  It is probably an original print.  She wears a fuchsia pink skirt with patent leather fascia pink shoes to match.  Her hair is cut short – a pixy cut and so silver it would give sterling a run for its money.  She is a very well put together old woman.  One wonders what she looked like in her younger years.

Dan is surprised by all the state-of-the-art computers in the library.  There are only four but at least they have them.  He introduces himself to the old librarian.

In a whisper, "Hi, my name is Dan Seagirt."

She introduces herself, "I'm Ms. Owens.  What can I help you with?"

"I'm looking for articles on the history of Blytheville.  Not 100 years ago," he chuckles, "but maybe the last 25 years."

"Okay, well we'll have to go to microfiche to find what you are looking for."  She comes out from behind the big wood desk and tells Dan to follow her.

"If you look through these files you will see a number at the top right.  This is the microfiche number.  Take a piece of paper and a pencil and write down the numbers.  You should also write down the page number, column and line numbers as well.  They will help you when you are looking through the microfiche.  Bring the number to me and I will pull the appropriate microfiche for you."  She starts walking off again so Dan quickly follows her.  She's moves pretty fast for her age.

"Then you come over here and sit down. Take the microfiche and place it here on the screen. Then turn the machine on with this button here." She's pointing to everything as she provides instruction. "This is the knob that will help you focus the articles. You can feed the microfiche through the machine with this button. Be careful because it moves very fast."

Dan looks at the machine and remembers his high school library. This machine must be 20 years old. It's amazing that things don't change.

Ms. Owens continues, "There is paper here if you want to write anything down or you can press this button here and print the page you are looking at. Once you are finished, you need to bring the microfiche back to me. This is very important. Do not leave them in the machine."

Dan smiles, "Of course not. I will bring them back to you."

"If you need any help I'll be at my desk," she says as she quickly walks off.

Over the course of the next two months, Dan works with Ms. Owens and interviews numerous people in town. He spends hours with Ms. Owens, tapping into her memory, but she's of no help in his quest. He does enjoy her company, though. She brings him in a piece of pie everyday and they sit and eat pie and drink a cup of coffee together. Dan meets several people who remember graduation day and what happened to Cyrus. No one has any answers; just that he collapsed from stomach pain and was taken to the hospital. That is the last anyone heard of Cyrus.

Dan tries to find Cyrus's mom but word on the street is she hooked up with some drug runner and left town years ago. Cyrus's sister followed in his mom's footsteps and turned to the profession of stripping. She was young when Cyrus collapsed and doesn't remember much of anything. All of Dan's leads are officially dried up, except for one, a guy named Mike Chambers.

Ms. Owens remembers that Mike, Cyrus and John were inseparable. She rarely saw them in the library as they weren't the studious types but she did recall seeing them around the school from time to time. Dan asks her about Mike and where he could find him. The librarian points him in the direction of past articles. She remembers Mike was a football player and got a scholarship to some university. She points him to where the article files are.

# Chapter 15

It is a beautiful sunny day, perfect for a party. All of the tables are out with white linens, white wood folding chairs under a white canopy. Each place setting is perfect; one large white plate; one small white plate; and a silver fork and spoon sitting on top of a light fuchsia yellow napkin. Ten large dark, 10 light yellow and three dark green balloons are tied in a bundle to each leg of the canopy. In the center of each table is an eight-inch white ice sculpted swan. Inside the back of the swan is a mix of flowers—one lily, one yellow rose, one yellow hibiscus and one purple hydrangea. They explode from the back of a swan like the feathers of a bird. These are the last items to be put out before the party starts.

The cake is three tiers of vanilla cake with light and dark chocolate icing. Each layer has a hand painted C on the top in the center, for Chambers. The cake is placed on the table in the center under the canopy. There is a stage erected at the end of the canopy for the band. The stage is covered with a white carpet that displays a large yellow "C" in the center.

Mike's home is in one of the nicer neighborhoods in Atlanta. The homes were built in the early 1900 but remain stylish and clean. Sadie helped Mike choose it after he was drafted by the Atlanta Falcon's. When you drive up to the home there are several large trees lining the front, only stopping for the driveway. The driveway is 1,000 feet long so you can't see the house from the street. It's not a straight drive but curvy so that you can enjoy the grounds before you get to the house. In the front of the house are several acres of fresh cut green grass, perfectly manicured. In the center is a garden full of roses, azaleas and oleanders. This is one of Sadie's favorite aspects of the house.

The house is all red brick with four large white stone columns in front. There are windows that line the second floor but the one that catches your eye is the window over the front door. It's almost two stories high, with the most exquisite Swarovski crystal chandelier hanging in the center. It's hard to notice anything else. When you walk into the home you see the Cinderella staircase, which was built wide enough that four people could walk up or down together. It curves up to the landing on the second floor, leading hallways that take you to five separate bedrooms. Each bedroom is large, with its own bathroom. The houses of this time period were built for parties just like this.

Sadie is less excited than she expected. Today is Mike's parents' thirtieth anniversary. The only joy of the day is that Cynthia is coming. She flew in from New York with Jerry and the baby. The new mom is loaded with stories of her exciting life; she can't wait to fill Sadie in on all the excitement. Sadie hired a big band to play all the oldies.

"Sadie, it looks gorgeous." Cynthia says as she gives her a big hug.

"Oh, thanks. This was such a pain in the ass to pull together. Mike didn't do a thing, of course. He hired some bitch to plan it and she called me with all of her questions. Like I have nothing better to do."

"Come on Sadie. They're his parents."

"Yeah, I know. But I had to help plan the party, fly all their friends in, make hotel arrangements, you know. His sister should have taken care of this. She didn't even bother to show up."

"Sadie, she's eight months pregnant."

"Oh, yeah. I'm sorry. That's one of those mother things I wouldn't know about." Sadie scans the crowd as she talks with Cynthia. "Look at all of them, the wives. Mike made me invite them all and they only talk to each other. They never speak to me. I'm just 'the girlfriend'."

"Well, why don't we go sit at their table—you know, mingle a bit."

"No, thanks. I have to sit with them when I go to a game. That's enough."

"Wow, what happened to the sweet Sadie? You have gotten really bitter since college."

"It's not bitter, I'm just over it."

"Well, I'm going to go sit down with Jerry. I suggest you have a drink, a strong one, and get in a better mood."

Sadie just smiles and walks off, heading for the bar.

"I'll have a Kettle One, three ice cubes and a lemon wedge, please."

"Okay Ms...?" The bartender says inviting a response.

"Call me Sadie. I'm not that old yet!"

The bartender just gives her a curious look.

She grabs her drink and walks off. She actually started drinking earlier in the day in preparation for the party. The food is being served. An hour later the band starts to play and people start to get up and dance, with Mike's parents leading the way.

Mike walks over to Sadie, "Hi gorgeous, would you like to dance?"

"I don't know, I mean, you're a professional athlete. I don't know if I could keep up with you." She says with slurring sarcasm.

"Great, you're drunk. Maybe I'll get lucky tonight." Mike grabs her hand and pulls her out of her chair.

"I wouldn't hold my breath."

By 10:00 p.m. the crowd begins to thin.

"Hey Sadie, I'm going to take the baby in and put her down. She's needs a quieter place to sleep." Cynthia says.

"Okay, sweetie," Sadie smiles. "I'll be in soon. We can catch up."

"Maybe tomorrow, I think you'll be passed out soon."

"Okay, whatever." Sadie turns back and looks out at the dance floor. Her head is placed firmly in the palm of her hand and her eyes are beginning to close.

By 11:00 the crowd is gone and the cleaning crew is working through the mess. Mike walks over to the table; Sadie is still in the same position she was an hour ago.

"Honey, come on. The party's over." He nudges Sadie and her head falls out of her hand.

"What, what happened?" She says as she looks around.

"The parties over babe, let's go inside. Mom and Dad went to the hotel to have a night cap with their friends. It's just you and me." He smiles.

Sadie just looks up at him with a blank stare.

"Well, I guess it's just me," he says as he picks her up and carries her upstairs.

In the morning everyone is downstairs having coffee and pastries when Sadie finally gets up. She's moving very slow. Mike left her a bottle of water and aspirin by the bed with a note that says "Take the pills and a shower and come down for breakfast...or lunch."

Mike and Susan are sitting on the patio.

"How's everything with Sadie?" Susan asks.

"It's good, things are great. She's better now that she graduated law school. Not so stressed, you know. We just moved all of her stuff in."

"Is she still planning on going into criminal law?"

"She's been talking about it. I think she really gets into it, working with all of those crooks and thieves. I was surprised at first but she actually gets them, you know. She understands where they're coming from. That's why she will be really good at it."

"Okay Mike, you know her best. Oh, that reminds me; I meant to tell you. Remember your friend John?"

"John Gillman from high school?"

"Yes, John Gillman. Well, he's been living in New York going to NYU Law and had some sort of a seizure and went into a coma. His parents brought him back a few months or so ago. The doctors in New York weren't helping and they needed to get back home so they moved him. We should ask Sadie if she knows him."

"Oh my God. A seizure? Does anyone know from what?"

"They don't know. They're having some specialist from California run some tests next month. The poor boy. His roommate is coming with them. He's a reporter in New York and he's been trying to help figure out what happened."

"Wow. That's too bad. I haven't talked to him since we graduated."

"Yep, well now you may never talk to him again."

"Mom! That's awful; and no time to joke"

"Well it's true. It's just like Cyrus. You know they finally had to move him to an assisted living facility. He just lies there, even after all these years. That boy's never gonna wake up."

"Mom, that's enough. You're depressing me. This is all so morbid!"

Sadie walks in, "What are you two talking about?"

"Just some people I knew from high school," Mike says. "Are you feeling okay?"

"I'm okay, a little hung over. You've never mentioned anyone from high school before. Who are they?"

"No one, just a couple of guys I was buddies with in high school. They're both in the hospital in a coma. Not together of course. It's sort of weird that they both ended up in the hospital and are both in a coma."

"You never know Mike, you have to take care of yourself," his mom says. "You have a dangerous job and you should think about retiring!"

"I've been playing for two years, Mom! I don't think I'm ready to retire yet. I'd like to get married and have a family first," he says, looking right at Sadie.

Sadie ignores him completely. "Susan's right, Mike; you might want to think about retiring. You don't want to wait until you get hurt." Sadie turns to Susan and asks, "Do you know what happened to his friends?"

Mike interrupts, "What do you mean, Sadie? You can't catch a coma. Anyway, what happened to Cyrus was almost seven years ago. Everyone knows he was a drug addict. And don't get on the retiring band wagon, Sadie. I'm only 24, and what will I do if I retire?" Mike snaps. "It's not like I have kids to see grow up."

"Stop with the marriage attacks on Sadie, Mike. You can't pressure her into marrying you." Susan pauses for a moment. She has never taken Sadie's side on this issue. "You could always go into finance. That's what you went to college for, and it's safer." His mom snaps back.

"I think I'll wait for a few more years, if you two don't mind," he says as he walks into the kitchen to hang out with his dad.

"I wouldn't worry about those boys from high school. Cyrus was always in trouble and it was probably drugs with him. I heard a rumor that John is a...you know...homosexual. It probably has something to do with that and his parents just don't want people to know," Susan says. "You know, he really should quit football though, Sadie! He takes a risk every time he walks out onto that field."

"I know, you're right. I wish he would quit but he loves to play football." Sadie says as she secretly gives a wily smile.

"I know, and he's stubborn, just like his father. His friend John Gillman was at NYU Law School. Do you know him?"

"Ha!'" Sadie laughs at how little Susan knows about New York City. "Doesn't sound familiar. I didn't know all the students in New York City, Susan. It's a big city! And I was a Columbia, which is a long way from NYU."

"Well, I'm sure you'll hear about it from one of your school friends at some point. They must talk in the law student community"

Sadie chuckles again. "Yes, they do. So sad, though. Maybe Mike should go visit him."

"He won't do that. They haven't spoken in years. You know, between you and me, I think Mike was glad to break away from them."

"Why would you say that?"

"Oh, I don't know. It was like he wanted out of Blytheville as soon as he realized where he lived, but it got worse when he was in high school. Too small of a town for him, I guess."

"Yeah, small town, small town people I guess." Sadie starts to walk towards the family room. "You know, I'm going to go see how Cynthia and the baby are. You don't mind, do you?"

"No, go ahead." Susan responded, still in her own thoughts about Mike.

Sadie finds Cynthia sitting in a chair in the family room feeding the baby.

"Hey, how's it going?" Cynthia asks.

"I can't wait for this day to end!" She replies as she sits next to Cynthia on the couch.

"What's wrong, sweetie?"

"Everything, nothing. I'm tired of Mike and his parents. Always talking about football, why we aren't married, what's going on in my life, high school, and on and on."

"You can't blame them, Sadie. You guys have been together for a couple of years now. They expect you to get married. They want grandchildren."

"Mike's sister has that covered!"

Cynthia laughs, "Yes she does!"

"Why do we need to get married? Things are fine the way they are."

"Are they? I mean, you seem really unhappy, Sadie."

"I'm fine. I'm just tired. I just finished law school, for crying out loud."

"I know, sweetie. I know. And now you'll start your own career, and Mike has his career and there won't be much time for anything else."

"You mean kids. Just say it."

"Look, what's the worst thing that could happen, Sadie? You marry him, he continues to be the ass he always was and you divorce him and take half his shit."

They both burst out laughing.

"That doesn't sound so bad Cyn, not so bad at all!" Sadie's wily smile quickly returns.

# Chapter 16

Dan checks into the Sheraton in Atlanta. He is exhausted from the drive and in need of a shower. After cleaning himself up he locates Mike Chambers with the help of one of his NY1 colleagues.

The phone rings and Sadie picks up, "Hello?"

Dan delays a bit...his heart is racing and for once in his life, he's speechless.

"Hello?" repeats Sadie.

"Oh...Hi! My name is Dan Seagirt; I'm a reporter with NY1 in Manhattan. I'm doing a story on the NFL and quarterbacks and wondered if I could speak with Mr. Chambers."

"He's not home right now. But these types of things generally go through his publicist. You should contact them directly to set something up. Goodbye".

"No but...wait..." Shouts Dan.

Sadie has already hung up.

Dan rings back.

"Hello," says Sadie

"Hi, Ma'am, it's Dan again."

"Sir, I told you, you'll have to..."

"I know, but listen, please. This is very important."

"Go on."

"My boy...I mean, my friend, went to high school with your husband."

"Oh, really? And he is not my husband!"

"I'm sorry. I just...well anyway, yes my friend recently went into a coma and so..."

"Is that that John, what's his name...?"

"Yes, John. How did you know?"

"Mike's mother told us what happened. We are so sorry to hear about your friend."

"Thank you. It is devastating to say the least. I'm trying to reach Mike to ask him a few questions about another friend of theirs, Cyrus, who also is in a coma."

"Really? Well that seems odd now doesn't it?" Sadie pauses. "Listen, Mike is at practice right now. Maybe you should try to catch him directly."

"Good idea. I think I will try that. But I would like to leave my number in case I miss him. And would you mind terribly trying to phone him and let him know I'm coming?"

"No problem. I'll call him," Sadie says.

He gives Sadie his mobile number and the number to the Sheraton. It's still quite hot in Atlanta so Dan puts on a short sleeved white linen shirt with a pair of khaki pants. He grabs his keys and his bag and heads out of his room. Dan gets in his rented Ford Taurus and drives to the practice field.

The Concierge tells him where the field is. They also tell him that security is pretty tight so he shouldn't expect to talk to any of the players. Dan just ignores the warning and takes off to find the practice field.

Sadie calls Mike and gets through.

"Hey, I wanted to let you know some guy from NY1 called, he wanted to talk to you. He's a friend of John Gillman's. He said he thinks there's a connection between what happened to John and your other friend Cyrus." Sadie says.

When he hears the words, Mike's stomach drops. He immediately starts to panic. Did they find Ellen? Do they know? Why would someone want to talk to him about Cyrus and John? Then he remembers that they are both in a coma so maybe this is about that. Maybe they want to warn him, or maybe this is the person responsible for Cyrus and John. Mike can't concentrate. Sadie is still talking and he hasn't heard a word.

"Mike, are you listening to me. Hello! What's wrong with you? I know you're not the smartest guy in the world but you understand English, right?"

"What honey, what did you say? I'm sorry. My mind is somewhere else. Practice is starting, I gotta go!" Mike hangs up on Sadie.

Sadie, pissed from her conversation with Mike, calls Dan and lets him know she talked to Mike. She tells him that Mike really wants to talk to him. This is a complete lie but she says it anyway. Mike deserves it for hanging up on her.

The practice field is on the outskirts of Atlanta. There is a field with a 10-foot fence surrounding it. A freshly laid black track circles the field; several of the players are running laps. The field is regulation size, with practice equipment on one end and players running drills on the other. There is a small set of stands on the other side of the field, most likely for the coaches to sit and talk while the players practice. On the sidelines are tables set up with water, Gatorade, football equipment, playbooks and extra jerseys. As Dan walks closer to the field he notices the security guards standing at the entrance. There are six of them and each looked like a retired front lineman for the team. Dan grabs his reporter's credentials before he left for Blytheville, luckily, so he pulls them out of his bag. They are attached to a string which he puts around his neck. As he gets closer he can't believe it—the guards actually looked larger! This isn't going to be easy.

"I'm sorry, sir, no reporters allowed on the practice field," one of the large guards announces.

"Oh, I know. Don't worry. I wanted to wait for Mr. Chambers to finish with practice and then interview him. He knows I'm here, I talked to his wife, Sadie."

"Well practice won't be over for another hour so you need to go back to your car and wait."

169

An hour's a long time and Dan doesn't have anything else to do. He decides to ask these guys some questions, maybe find out what it's like to do their job; he has nothing else to talk to them about.

"Well, I thought I might ask you guys a few questions while I am waiting. You see I'm doing a story on NFL quarterbacks and all the folks that help make them successful. Like you guys. You keep him safe while he's practicing so he can focus. Do you mind?" he asks as he pulls a tape recorder out of his pocket.

"Yes, we mind," snaps one of the guards.

"Hey, speak for yourself, you, I don't mind a few questions," says another guard. "Go ahead and ask me your questions."

"Great!" Now what is he going to do, he has no questions prepared. "Let's see, I need to get my questions out of my bag." Dan starts sifting through his bag for a pad, killing time so he could think of what he is going to ask this rather large man for an hour.

"So you obviously played football, right?"

"Yeah, I played center in college. Hurt my shoulder my junior year."

"You must have has a tight relationship with the quarterback then?"

"Yeah, tight like a Gatorade cap, man; I protected his ass!" He laughs and gives a high five to one of the other security guards.

"Yeah, Gatorade cap, that's a good one. So do you think the same relationship exists on the Falcons?"

"They seem to get along pretty well, right, Sam?" He turns to a fellow guard and asks.

"Yeah man, they're tight," Sam says, sitting on a table paying no attention to what is going on.

"So do you guys get to interact with these guys much?"

"Nah, they come in, practice, shower and leave. They don't say much to anybody."

"Except those cheerleaders, yo," one of the guards chimes in with a chuckle. "Them girls is hot!"

"Look, these are professional athletes. They don't have time for anything," says the guard who doesn't want to be interviewed. "What are they going to talk to us about? You need to go wait in your car!"

"Dude, what is wrong with you? You're always trying to act like you're in charge, yo. You ain't in charge of shit. You don't have to go anywhere; you just keep asking me whatever you want to, man."

Dan is starting to get nervous. These guys are big and he doesn't need to get in the middle of their fight.

"You sure it's okay? I can go wait in my car, it's not a problem."

"No man, I say you can stay here. Now what else you want know?"

"Well, do you just work during the off season or do you guys travel with the team?"

"Just the off season, man."

171

"Okay. How many people try to get into meet these guys during practice?"

"Oh, we get at least four or five every practice. There's always some idiot that thinks these guys are just sitting around waiting to sign footballs!" He laughs and a couple of the other guards laugh with him.

"Is it usually kids or adults?"

"It's usually some ass who wants to sell the shit on eBay!"

"Yeah, I heard that is a big complaint with the players."

"Yeah, it is. You think you're signing a ball for a fan and it's some jackass trying to make a buck off your name."

"So what do you do with them?"

"We throw their ass out," he says as he high fives a couple of the guys.

"Good thing I don't have a football, right?" Dan tries to laugh but it is obvious he is nervous.

"Naw man, you're okay, little man. We won't hurt you...yet!" They all laugh out loud.

Dan notices the players starting to gather around the coach and starts to walk off.

"Hey, what are you doing man?" one of the guards yells.

"Okay, you gotta go. No problem man, make sure you spell my name right! R. A. Y. B. E. N. D. E. R!" He turns to his fellow guards, "You know that guy swings the other way right!" They all laugh.

"You are the one that wanted to talk to him, man, you thinking of trying out something new, Ray," laughs Sam.

"Yeah, I'll show you something new, yo" he says as he grabs his crotch. They all laugh.

Dan glances at a picture he printed of Mike to make sure he gets the right guy. All the players have their helmets on so Dan has a hard time locating him. He tries to alter his position so he can get a better look at their faces as they run into the locker room, but it's of no help. One by one the players exit the locker room, passing Dan at the gate. Finally Mike appears and as he passes Dan, Dan yells…

"Hey, Mike. Mike Chambers. Can I talk to you? My name is Dan. Your wife told you about me?"

Mike looks at him and quickly turns and rushes off, trying to avoid him. He acts like his wife didn't mention it, but she did. Dan knows Sadie talked to him because she told him she did. She would have no reason to lie. Dan wonders why Mike is ignoring him.

Mike jumps into his Mercedes S500 and speeds off. Dan follows him. It isn't easy. He isn't familiar with the area and he is in a Ford Taurus. Mike pulls up to his home, which of course has a big gate in front. The gate is attached to a security system and a brick wall that outlines the perimeter. Dan pulls ahead and parks on the street, waiting for Mike to get into the house. He gives him 20 minutes and then calls the house.

"Hello," says the female voice again.

"Hi, this is Dan, I called earlier. I wanted to see if Mr. Chambers has gotten home from practice."

"Oh, hello again. Yes, he's here. Hold on a minute." She hands Mike the phone. "It's that reporter I tried to tell you about earlier when you hung up on me."

Mike barks, "I don't want to talk to him...not now...I'm not feeling well. Tell him I'll call him tomorrow."

Sadie does, reluctantly, but Dan is relentless and aggressive. Sadie is forced to hang up on him but not before she gives him Mike's mobile number. Mike thinks to himself that Sadie is enjoying this. She's trying to get him back for hanging up on him.

Dan drives back to the hotel, angry and frustrated. He starts wondering what Mike has to hide. In the morning he gets a call from Sadie. She tells him that Mike goes to the same diner every morning for breakfast and then hangs up. When Dan arrives at the diner Mike is in blue sweats and a t-shirt. His hair is still wet from his morning shower. He is eating his breakfast as if a dog is sitting next to him waiting for the food to fall from the plate. Dan walks up to his booth. The diner is shaped like a train car, silver with a big neon sign. The front is lined with windows, all one after the other. When you walk through the front door bells attached to the door handle ring. Inside there is a bar with a red linoleum counter and red stools. The stools are attached to the floor. There are booths that line the inside walls, red fake leather seats and red linoleum tables. In the center are the same red tables and metal chairs.

"Good morning," Dan says. "You must be Mike?"

"Hey," Mike says as he put his fork down and swallowing the food in his mouth. "Good morning."

"Can I sit down?"

"Um no. Who the hell are you and why would I let you sit with me? Beat it?"

Dan insists, telling Mike his story and mentioning John. Mike has no recourse but to allow it. Mike offers him something to eat, much to his dismay.

"Not really, I think I'll just have coffee." The waitress notices Dan at Mike's table. They always keep an eye on Mike when he is there. She comes over and asked Dan if he wants to see the menu. He tells her he just wants coffee.

"So you work for NY1?" Mike asks.

"Yes. I started working for them when I was in college and I'm still there."

"What exactly do you want?"

"I want to talk to you about Cyrus and John. I mean, don't you think it's funny that your two best friends from high school are both in a coma?"

"Yeah, I guess. I never really thought about it." Mike is feeling nervous and wondering if Dan can tell. "We did get into some trouble. I mean, Cyrus was really into drugs. We just all assumed he took something before graduation and overdosed."

"Yeah, but now with John I'm not so sure."

"Why, what does John have to do with Cyrus?"

"I don't know, that's what I'm trying to figure out."

"Why? What's it to you?"

"John was my boyfriend and I loved him very much. I just can't let it go. It doesn't make any sense. Healthy young men don't just slip into a coma for no reason."

"Well, didn't the doctor tell you why?"

"Yeah, they rationalize it with maybe it was this, or maybe it was that, but they don't really know."

"I'm sorry man, really I am. I just don't know what this has to do with me." Mike was feeling better now. Dan had no idea, he was fishing. He didn't know about Sadie.

"Well, if it is connected, aren't you worried? I mean, who's to say it won't happen to you?"

Mike laughed. "Dude, come on. A conspiracy, involving three guys from Blytheville. You don't really believe that do you?"

Dan put his face in his hands and shook his head. "I don't know what I believe anymore. To hear you say it does seem silly."

"Yeah, silly. Look, I am really sorry about John, man, but I gotta go, I can't be late. It was nice talking to you, Dan. I hope John comes out of it." Mike stands up, throws a $20 on the table and heads out the door.

Dan starts to get up to go after him but it is no use. Mike doesn't know anything and Dan's feeling foolish now because he has no reason to be asking any questions. Dan stares out the window, watching Mike leave. He wonders if it is really that simple, a drug-using kid takes one drug too many and his body freaks out. Maybe it is. Maybe he is being paranoid; maybe he is too close to the situation to be objective.

The waitress comes back over to see if he is hungry but he has completely lost his appetite. He gets up and walks out to his car. He sits in his car for a few minutes thinking about what to do next. He has no leads and John is still lying in a coma in the hospital. His heart sinks at the thought of John. He should go back and be with him. At some point he is going to have to make the decision about going back to New York. He has to get back to work. The office has been calling him and asking him when he is coming back. He tries to be objective. At this point all the data is gathered, evaluated and assessed. Nothing pointed to any kind of connection or foul play. He just can't accept that this is happening to him; he is losing John and he can do nothing about it.

When he gets back to the hotel he packs up his bags. Maybe this is the closure he is looking for, the end to his personal drama. He checks out of the hotel and gets in his car to head back to Blytheville. He needs to go and say goodbye to John. He asks himself, "Can I really let this go?"

Mike goes home after practice and Sadie is waiting for him with dinner.

"Hi honey, how was practice?"

177

"Good sweetie," he says as he grabs her around the waist and kisses her cheek.

"So how was breakfast this morning?" Sadie asks as she serves dinner.

"Did you tell him where I would be?" Mike says annoyed. "You did, didn't you?" He looks over at her and sees the smile on her face. "I knew it. Thanks a lot, Sadie. Sometimes I think you hate me!"

"Oh Mike, don't be so dramatic. He's friends with John, and I guess trying to find out if there's a connection between Cyrus and John and their comas. Were you able to help him out? It's so sad...."

"It was fine...a very interesting guy."

"What do you mean, interesting? Weird interesting on good interesting?"

"Weird interesting. He kept asking me about high school."

"High school? That is weird. Why would he ask about high school? You've been out of high school forever," Sadie says with a high pitch, as if the years were piling up.

"Thanks hun. I feel real young and spry!"

"I'm sorry," Sadie says, "I meant....well...you know what I mean. High school was ages ago."

"Again, with the 'age' thing" says Mike.

"Hun, I'm just giving you shit now."

"Oh, sorry." said Mike

"Okay, back to the interview. What happened exactly? Walk me through it." said Sadie

"This guy kept asking me about my friends and stuff. I told him I don't talk to anyone from high school. I don't even go back for reunions. He told me the kids back home will benefit from me going back, someone to look up to, you know?

"Uh-huh." Sadie places Mike's plate of food on the table, "Go on."

"He's probably right, I never really thought about the fact that I'm probably a role model for people back home, ya know? I mean, I'm sure a lot of my friends think I'm a jerk because I just left and never looked back." Mike says all smug.

"Well, maybe there's that," Sadie says under her breath.

"I mean, the whole conversation did make me think about an old buddy of mine, Cyrus."

"Oh yeah? That's nice. Old friends are good."

"And so is this lasagna." Mike says as he smacks Sadie on the ass. "You want some of this?" he says with a flirty smirk.

"Hardly. I'd like to hear the rest of the story. Maybe you'll get some later," said Sadie.

"All right, I'll take your word for it. So anyway, this guys' bringing up high school and I start thinking about a buddy I had, this guy Cyrus. A real character. I haven't thought about him in a long, long time." says Mike.

"I've never heard you mention him before," says Sadie as she picks at her food.

Mike says, "I know I've never mentioned him before, that's what I'm saying, I totally forgot about him until today. Yeah, he was an old friend of mine. And man, did we get into some trouble." Mike stares off into space, thinking about the good old days. But his face quickly goes from smiling to worry as his mind also remembers what they did to that girl.

"Well then, it's probably a good thing you don't keep in touch with him." Sadie says.

"Yeah, well, I couldn't if I wanted to. He's been in a hospital since we graduated. He had some sort of reaction and has been in a coma since. If he's even still alive, which I don't know because I haven't been in touch."

"A coma? How awful. I can't believe you've never told me about this friend of yours. What happened to him?" Asked Sadie

"I don't know. Probably drugs. He liked to mess around with drugs. If it weren't for football I would have, too. Like I said, I haven't thought about him for years." Mike's easiness turns to worry and he quickly shuts the conversation down. "Anyway, I don't want to talk about it anymore. It is old news and I've moved on."

In a sexy voice he reaches across the table and puts his hand on Sadie's chin, "My beautiful, smart lady who's gonna give me some tonight!"

"Not so fast" says Sadie. "I'm a little tired."

"Tired? What? C'mon hun. You say that every night".

"Sorry hunny. I'm really tired and not in the mood" says Sadie.

"But what happened to being in the mood before dinner? C'mon hun. A man needs some lovin'," says Mike, distressed.

And as Sadie clears the table she says in an annoyed manner, "Not gonna happen. End of story. I need to do some work before my trip in a couple days.

"Jesus Sade...this is getting to be ridiculous. You haven't touched me or let me touch you in months. It feels like a goddamned year." Mike says

"It's gonna be a lot longer if you don't get off my back about it."

"I can't even imagine!" Mike says angrily and walks out of the room.

# Chapter 17

The drive back to Blytheville seems to take days instead of hours. It is the longest drive of Dan's life. How do you tell someone you love goodbye? He is struggling and knows it will only get worse when he gets to the hospital. He has to go, he has to say goodbye and move on with his life.

He arrives at the hospital right before dark. He goes to the nurse's station; they know Dan well at this point. He asks to see John and they agree. They can tell from his demeanor that this is the end; they know Dan has come to say goodbye.

When Dan walks into the room he sees John. He looks the same. Lying lifeless in his bed hooked up to several machines. They removed the ventilator; John could breathe on his own now. The vibrant law student and class president is gone. All that is left is this shell; a shell that holds the man he once loved. He walks over to the chair and moves it close to the bed. He sits down and reaches up to hold John's hand. He starts to weep. He puts John's hand to his mouth and kisses the inside. His tears are rolling down his face into John's hand. There is no reaction from John.

"What am I supposed to do without you? I can't go back to our home, I can't work, and it's just not the same without you. I tried to figure out what happened, John, I tried. Wake up! Please wake up."

There is no movement from John. His coma is deep and endless. There is no brain activity, which means no hope. The doctors have been very clear about that. John is going to be in this coma until his body quits.

Dan sits with John for two hours, sobbing and saying goodbye. He falls asleep at one point, lying in the bed with John, when the nurse comes in. She wakes him up gently and tells him it is time to go. Dan takes one long last look at John as he slowly walks out of the room. This will be the last time he will ever see John.

# Chapter 18

Mike's dream of going to the championships and bringing home
that trophy ring has come. His team is going to the playoffs as the leader
of their division and analysts have been picked Atlanta as the next Super
Bowl Champions. Sadie agrees to marry him after the season is over.

Getting engaged finally lets Mike focus on nothing but football,
which has given Sadie a little breathing room from Mike's pestering.
And it's just as well because Sadie hasn't been around much anyway.
Her clients are keeping her busy.

December 21, 11:00 a.m. A stadium filled with screaming
Falcon fans is bursting with energy. It's the Falcons against the New
Orleans Saints. The Falcons have the home-field advantage. Mike is
pumped. The locker room is roaring with testosterone as the Falcons
huddle up for one last team moment before hitting the field. The crowd
of young men scream, "Ready, break!" and one by one they run out of
the locker room and onto the field.

Sadie is in the stands cheering amid the thousands of other
Falcon fans. The energy is high. The game begins with a burst of red,
gold and white fireworks. A layer of smoke hangs over the stadium
while country music blares over the loudspeakers. As the teams go onto
the field the fans go crazy. The announcers ask everyone to stand for the
national anthem; the flag bearers are on the field ready. They've invited
local heroes who have returned from Iraq to join them on the field. They

are dressed in their ceremonial uniforms, carrying a book with the names of all the soldiers who have lost their lives in the war.

The fans have been tailgating all morning, waiting for the game to start. Tim McGraw walks onto the field where the microphone is standing. He sings the National Anthem and when he finishes, the team captains and referees meet in the center of the field. Atlanta wins the coin toss and chooses to receive.

The Saints' kicker is in position. He pushes back; the ball is hiked, placed in the hands of the holder. And the kicker rushes as fast as he can. He hits the ball so hard it goes to just about the Atlanta 10 yard line. The crowd roars with excitement. The game is on.

"This should be a tough match-up today," says John Madden.

"You know, if the Falcon's defense can keep the Saints from passing the ball they should have an easy time moving on to the next game," answers Troy Aikman. "I'm not so sure, Troy. The Saints have a decent running game. They're a passing team but when they need 10 yards they can run the ball."

"Yeah. But 10 yards isn't gonna be enough today, John. The Falcons score an average of 25 points a game, so the Saints are gonna have to come with more than that."

"Let's see how it plays out then."

The Falcon's box is on the second level of the stadium. There are three rows of seats, plenty for the wives and their families. At the top of the seats is a bar with eight bar stools. Behind the bar is an L-shaped table with several types of food and drinks. There are hot dogs, chicken fingers, several varieties of pasta and salads. The dessert is displayed on big white dishes with the Atlanta Falcons logo in the center. There are two servers who keep the food replenished and the box cleaned up.

The first half is coming to an end and Atlanta is up 21 to 0. It is a great first half for Mike and the Falcons. The announcers can't get over the Falcon's performance.

"Let's replay that play again," says Madden.

"Again? Haven't you seen it enough times, John?" Troy jokes. "You'd think you were in love with Chambers!" Everyone in the announcer's box laughs and Madden turns a mild shade of red.

"I just appreciate talent, Troy, you know a good quarterback!" Madden says, poking fun at Troy. Troy doesn't find it too funny but he lets it go.

"Play the blasted tape, already," grunts Troy. "He's gonna just keep at it until we do."

As they go through the key plays of the first half and Madden adds his colorful commentary the players start to head back onto the field to warm up for the second half.

Sadie spends the break talking with a couple of other wives about her upcoming cases and the charities she is supporting. They talk about theirs as well. It is a role they know they can play, taking advantage of being married to a professional football player. Jessica turns to Sadie, who's talking with Gail about the American Heart Association benefit.

"So Sadie, isn't it great that we've held the Saints to a scoreless half? I mean, it only takes an interception to turn a game." She smiles.

"Yes, Jessica, I think the team is doing a great job tonight. Let's just hope they can keep it up in the second half." She walks off, smiling to herself. Jessica is a fool if she thinks she could ever make Sadie jealous. The game starts and Sadie is relieved from further conversation with Jessica.

"Here we go," says Sadie as she turns to look at the field.

Atlanta kicks off to the Saints. Even with the disadvantage at kickoff the Falcons quickly recover the ball and Mike runs it straight into the end zone for another touchdown.

During the quarter he has great success throwing the ball down the field to his top receiver, Ed. They quickly get to the Saints' 20 yard line. It is 3$^{rd}$ and 1 and Mike calls a quarterback sneak. He walks up to the line and places his hands in position under the nose guard. The ball is hiked and everyone on the line pushes forward with everything they have. Mike follows the nose guard; it feels like he's moving in slow motion. He gets hit hard by a lineman on the right, then again on the left. Someone pushes him from behind but instead of going forward he goes down hard to the field. His helmet hits the ground and he feels the turf on his face as his head slides across the ground. His lower body is following but before it can hit the ground he gets hit repeatedly.

Everyone piles on top. When the referees finally break the pile apart, Mike is left lying on the ground. He got the first down but he isn't moving. The coach and trainers are on the field.

One of the wives watching the game sees what's going on the field as Sadie continues to talk to some others about her work. The wife screams across the room, "Sadie, Mike's down on the field," she says.

Sadie turns to look at the field and very uncaring way says, "He'll get up, he always does."

They watch as the coach and trainer work on Mike. He gets up but limps off the field. He can't put any weight on his right leg. He's hurt the same knee he hurt in college. The announcers are replaying the hit.

"Take a look at that hit from 56, see how the knee bends as he's going down." Madden says, wincing.

"Yeah John, that had to hurt. He's not going to recover from a hit like that today. I'll be surprised if he comes back this season at all." Troy adds.

"That's too bad, Troy; Atlanta has a real shot at the Super Bowl. For a guy like Chambers...well he's not going to get a lot of opportunities like this one."

"You could be right, John, but you never know. I mean, QBs take hits..." Troy pauses as he looks at the hit again during a replay. "Like I was saying, we take hits and sometimes it looks a lot worse from up here than it really is."

"I don't know how it can look worse, Troy," Madden gives Troy a puzzled look. "Up here, down there, that hit hurts."

Sadie's not even looking at the field when Jessica says, "It looks like he's hurt Sadie, and maybe you should go down there."

"No, Mike wouldn't like that. I'm sure he's fine. They'll call up if it's serious."

A few of the wives look at her confused, as if she is being so cold-hearted.

"If it is serious they will call up to the box." says Sadie

They all watch as the second string QB, Johnson, runs out to the field and Mike is taken to the locker room.

"This isn't good," says Madden. "Atlanta's got to lose momentum with this switch."

"Yeah, Johnson hasn't had much playing time this year so I'm not sure that he can lead this team, John." Adds Troy.

"Well, he just needs to hold them through this half, keep the team moving up the field. If he can't do that then the Falcons could be in for a long afternoon."

"There is no real reason for concern, the Falcons have a good lead and the Johnson is a pretty good back-up," says Troy.

At the end of the 3$^{rd}$ quarter the score is 21 to 14. Mike sits on the sidelines with his knee wrapped while Johnson holds it together but they really need to score in the 4$^{th}$ quarter. After each series he calls

Johnson over to talk about the plays and work on a better strategy. Sadie can see the frustration on Mike's face as the cameras are on him constantly for his reactions. It is clear how badly he wants to be on the field. When his face comes on the Jumbotron the crowd chants, "Chambers, Chambers, Chambers." It makes Mike feel useless but proud that his fans support him.

The $4^{th}$ quarter isn't any easier than the $3^{rd}$. The Saints drive down the field like a powerhouse. This game has taken a serious turn in the Saints' favor. It takes everything the Falcons' defense has to keep them from scoring more than 14 points. The only positive is the interception the Falcon safety Bartlett makes in the Saints' red zone, which he runs in for a touchdown. The crowd roars. It shifts the momentum and the Falcons go on to score another touchdown, winning the game by 7. One game down, and another in a week. The next game won't be as easy; they have to play the Buccaneers, who have always proven to be a challenge. Mike will need to be healthy for that game and he knows it.

Mike heads to the whirlpool to ice his knee in the big stainless steel tub of injury, as they call it. It's in the back of the locker room with the injury table and other medical equipment. All the guys are changing in the center, sitting on the benches and throwing their dirty laundry into large piles. Each player takes a minute to head back and show Mike support. He appreciates it but isn't in the mood to hear it. He's sitting with his eyes closed and trying to mentally stop the pain when he hears someone come in. He doesn't move or open his eyes. He hears a lot of banging and sits up to see what's going on.

"What the hell," Mike says. He looks up and sees the side view of a young man walking out of the room carrying towels. It's not Steve, the regular towel boy.

"Hey, what are you doing? Are you even supposed to be in here?" Mike yells.

The person turns to Mike with his head down, "Hi Mike."

"Who are you, what are you doing in here?" Mike snips.

"I just want to be close to you Mike. You know I love you. You didn't think I was going to forget about what you did. I've been watching you all these years. You and your friends, the women you've been with. They weren't good enough for you Mike, none of them."

"What!" Mike jumps up and grabs his towel, forgetting about his knee. He screams from the pain that shoots up his leg. When he looks back up, the person is gone.

The coach comes in, "Everything okay, Mike? I heard you scream?"

"Yeah, I'm fine," he grimaces holding his knee. "Did you see her, I mean the towel guy, run out of here?"

"No, why?"

"Nothing," he sighs. "It's nothing."

Mike comes home several hours later. The team spent time after the game reviewing films to make corrections for the next game. Mike works with the trainer on his knee. When he gets home he is frustrated and tired from the drugs they gave him for the pain. The x-rays show a sprain so he is happy about that, but it is painful. He needs to stay off it as much as possible.

When Mike walks in Sadie is working at her computer in the office. He is on crutches so it is difficult to get into the front door. Sadie hears the noise from the office and gets up to go and see what is going on. She sees Mike struggling with his stuff and the crutches.

"Mike, why didn't you call and let me know you were here? You're going to wake the neighbors with all that noise. Give me your bag." She grabs his bag and puts it off to the side, then closes the door behind him.

He thinks about telling her about the "towel guy," who he recognized, when he thought about it, as Sarah from Blytheville, but he's too mad at her for not showing up in the locker room. "We watched video from the game and then I had to ice my knee down."

"How's your knee? Same knee again?"

"Not like you care but yes. And it's just a sprain but the doc says I have to stay off of it. He wants me to lie in bed for a couple weeks and not move if I want to even consider playing in the next game. How am I supposed to do that?"

"You're just going to have to do it Mike, or don't play in the game. And I don't appreciate the 'like you care' remark."

"Most girlfriends would have at least come to the locker room, Sadie. You know, see if I'm okay. Forget it. We both know not playing is not an option. I didn't get this far not to go to the Super Bowl, Sadie. This is what I play football for."

"I know, that's why I said you're just going to have to do it. We can get someone to help out and take care of you for the week."

"What about you? You can take care of me."

"I have work and a charity commitment Mike, you know that. I have to go out of town tomorrow, just a day trip." She has no intention of telling him where she is really going. He doesn't even know she has a father, let alone one that lives so close by.

"What! Your charity commitment can wait, Sadie. This is important. I thought it WAS important to both of us."

"Mike, even if I didn't have the charity stuff I still have my clients. It's a full-time job, you know. What's the big deal? We'll get someone to come and help out for a few days each week. And, Cynthia's coming. She and Jerry want to watch you in the playoffs and they might stay through Christmas."

"Whatever. It's fine. I'm tired. I'm going to go to bed. Are you coming?"

"Yes, just let me clean up okay. I'll bring your bag up."

"Thanks."

Sadie goes back into the office to finish planning her trip while Mike struggles his way to bed. Mike's lying on the bed just replaying the day, the locker room. "Why was she back? What did she want?" He thinks. "Perfect timing. Just in time to screw everything up!"

193

# Chapter 19

The next week drags by. Mike only moves from the bed to go to the bathroom. The team trainer is over every day checking on him and doing physical therapy. Sadie and Cynthia are in and out doing Christmas shopping. Sadie hires a nurse to help take care of him. Mike is determined to play in the game against the Buccaneers; there is no debating it with him. They trainer tells him they will wrap his knee and shoot him up with cortisone so he can deal with the pain but it might not be enough. Mike doesn't care. He is playing.

With the playoffs and Mike hurt Sadie has to manage everything for Christmas on her own, and there isn't a lot of time. She's relieved to have Cynthia around to help. Sadie has a Christmas tree delivered to the house and Mike watches while she decorates it. She isn't big on following all the other wives Southern customs of decorating the inside and outside of your home like a winter wonderland. A Christmas tree was enough, and she took great care decorating it.

The tree is covered in red and green lights with hand painted ornaments in every color. They are all round so there is uniformity to the tree but the colors are as vibrant as the sun in the sky. Sadie has been collecting these ornaments for years. She painstakingly searched all over the country and the Internet to find the perfect ornaments for the tree. Nell was very careful with each one. She loves Christmas and she loves decorating the tree, it reminds her of her mother. When the last ornament is hung they go to the fireplace to hang their stockings.

Sadie and Mike have the same stocking, red with green and white argyle. Very preppy and conservative. Once the stockings are hung, Sadie brings the pizza from the kitchen and they all sit around the tree for dinner. Mike forgets about his knee, the playoffs, and the Super Bowl, everything for one night.

After dinner Cynthia takes Nell up to bed and tucks her in. When she comes back downstairs Mike is asleep on the couch and Jerry in the chair. She and Sadie go into the office, which Sadie has turned into her gift-wrapping center. There is paper all over the floor, gifts stacked up along the wall and bows hanging from the desk and the chairs. They clean up a bit and chat about their college days. They take the gifts and place them all under the tree, while they finish their second bottle of wine.

Within days it is Christmas Eve. Cynthia and Jerry decide to leave and visit her parents for the holiday, as painful as that may be. They were trying to avoid it but her parents were relentless. They refuse to spend a holiday without their granddaughter. It is misery but it is family.

Today feels like just another sunny day in Atlanta but it is Christmas Eve. Mike's parents come down around 3:00 p.m. for dinner and to open presents with the family. Mike's sister would have come this year but she is eight months pregnant again and doesn't want to travel. His parents stay the night but leave in the morning to go and spend Christmas Day with her. Mike doesn't mind; he can't do anything, anyway, and they don't have children. This is a subject of many conversations and all with the same outcome. Sadie's not ready.

Sadie has dinner catered; she is just too busy to cook. They are having filet mignon, garlic beans, green salad with tangerine and walnuts, butternut squash and fresh baked rolls. Sadie orders Mike's favorite for dessert, key lime pie.

They spent the afternoon and evening talking about the holiday season, the playoffs, and opening presents. Mike's lying on the couch with his knee elevated which puts him in perfect book-reading position. It is a quiet Christmas Eve. Sadie cleans up the mess and goes into the office to get the presents for the morning and put them by the fireplace. When she is finished she stands back, grabs her glass of wine and sits staring at the tree for what feels like hours. What did Christmas really mean to her?

# Chapter 20

Sunday, December 27. It's 70 degrees and the sky is clear. The field has been perfectly groomed and the stadium seats are starting to disappear as fans take their seats. The players spread across the field to warm up, doing jumping jacks, a side-to-side shuffle and stretching. The field goal kicker is in the center of the field practicing kicks at different distances. Several of the players use this time to relax and play out the game in their head. Others just focus on warming up and getting limber. The coaches are on the sidelines working out the plays for the day. They check their ear pieces to make sure the connection is strong with the booth. You can feel the focus and the tension.

The Falcons are playing Tampa Bay in Atlanta. This is one thing Mike has to be happy about, playing at home. He knows the field and is comfortable playing in his stadium. Before the game he goes out on the field to throw the ball and test his knee out a bit. He feels pretty good; there is no pain, just a little twinge now and then. He is growing more confident every minute.

The players leave the field with about 15 minutes to game time and head back to the locker room. The music is turned on and blasts through the speaker system, '70s southern rock, started off by THE Steve Miller Band Joker. Sadie is in the player's box. Sadie's in jeans, a red three-quarter sleeved blouse and boots.

All the wives ask Sadie about Mike. They are very concerned. Sadie thinks their concern is more for themselves than for Mike. She knows how much they want to go to the Super bowl. She sees Mike out on the field; everything looks normal.

Jessica, of course has to make a comment, "So Sadie, it must make Mike feel better knowing the defense definitely came to play today." She looks over at the other wives and gives them a superior nod.

Sadie is tired and isn't in the mood for her crap and replies, "Yes Jessica, I'm sure the entire offense sleeps so much better knowing the defense will do all the work." She doesn't even look at Jessica as she replies.

The game starts with its normal hoopla, lights and the singing of the national anthem. This time they ask a local child star wannabe to sing. She is actually pretty good. She's a cute little girl. Her mom has dressed her in a pageant-type dress, which looks a little out of place. Jeans and a cute top with an Atlanta hat would have been just as nice. She has a great voice and really sings the hell out of the anthem. The next thing you know, the ball flies through the air to the Atlanta receiving team. The game begins. All the fans can do now is sit back and watch.

"Okay, here we go," Madden says. "You think Chambers can play today?"

"Well, they have him suited up so that means he's going to try," Troy says with a concerned look. "I think I would stay off the knee to be

199

ready for the Super Bowl but they may think they need him just to get there."

"And they would be right!" Madden laughs as he says it.

"Well, they certainly have a better chance," Troy agrees.

The first quarter is tense; the announcers are critical of Mike's every move. If he misses a receiver it is because of his knee. If he gets sacked it is because of his knee. Mike runs out of the pocket and throws a 30-yard pass and gets hit hard directly after the throw. The Falcon crowd goes quiet.

"Did you see that," Madden yells. "I don't think he's gonna get up from that one."

"I don't know. John, it was a hard hit but I think he's gonna be okay," Troy says looking intently at the field.

"If he does he's gonna have a concussion. Troy, you know a lot about concussions right?" Madden chuckles.

Troy just ignores him. "Look, he's getting up. I think he's okay…and without a concussion John!"

"Wow, I don't believe it. He's tougher than I thought."

"He is a quarterback, John." Troy smiles.

Mike knows everyone is judging him but he doesn't care. The second quarter starts with the Falcons up 14 points. The crowd is on their feet as the first play begins. Mike is on fire, throwing the ball, running the ball, a few reverses and numerous audibles.

It's 3 and 12. Mike gets up to the line and gets ready to call the play. He sees the defense make a shift and immediately readjusts. The crowd just watches as they try to figure out what he's doing. The ball is in Mike's hands. The running backs behind him charge the line to help block as they play shifts from a run to a pass. Mike has one receiver and a tight end to work with. He doesn't see anyone open but there's a 330 pound linebacker coming after him. He turns and heads out of the pocket to the right. The linebacker is taken out by a Falcon. He hits the ground hard. Mike's pumping his arm, looking for an open receiver when he sees it. A hole as big as Kansas. He darts off his back right foot and heads into the hole like a tornado. By the time the Saints figure out what he's doing it's too late. He's runs 10 yards and is heading out of bounds with a 15 yard run. The fans go crazy and start chanting his name. No one expected him to run.

"Can you believe it?" Madden screams. "He ran the ball."

"Yeah, quarterbacks do that, John." Troy smirks.

"I know but he's hurt. He took a huge risk running that ball. Let's look at it again!"

"It doesn't look like his knee's hurting him at all now," says Troy.

They watch the play again, putting it up on the Jumbotron so the fans can enjoy it as well.

Mike continues to use all of his tools, everything he can to win the game. Every time he is hit the crowd holds their breath. He gets up every time. The second quarter ends and the Falcons have managed to hang on to their 14-point lead. They leave the field for the locker room.

"Mike, man, what a run," Ed says as he slaps Mike on the back.

"Thanks, man," Mike smiles.

"I mean, you didn't run that fast before you hurt your knee." Ed laughs.

"Nice, Ed."

The coach comes in and starts to talk with them about changes for the second half.

"Mike's doing good, Sadie; he looks great," says Ed's wife, Sharon.

Sharon is a true professional football player's wife. She has platinum blonde hair that she teases and twists to death. Her makeup is always exquisite; she never leaves home without her false lashes perfectly in place. She has an expensive set of implants a bit too large for her small frame. Maybe if she ate more than once a week they might look more proportionate. She shops at Barneys and only wears certain designers. Sharon always makes sure you know who she is wearing. Sadie has absolutely nothing in common with her but Ed and Mike are best friends so she is forced to be nice.

"Oh thanks, Sharon. He stayed off the knee for two weeks, doing physical therapy every day to get ready for the game."

"Ed told me. We need Mike to go to the Super Bowl, you know!"

"I know and so does he. I think he will have to be dead not to play."

Sharon laughs. "I hate to say it, but I think you're right."

The half is over and everyone is back in their seats. Mike jogs out as if he is 18 years old again. You would never know how much pain he was in just one week ago. The Falcons are back on the field to get ready for the kickoff. They kick the ball down the field; the special team front line is on the 20 in less than two seconds. They hit the ball carrier and the ball goes flying. Within a second one of the Falcon's grabs the ball and is heading for the end zone. They score. The crowd goes crazy! *TOUCHDOWN* flashes on the big screens and the music roars through the loudspeaker. They lead by 21.

As the quarter progresses the Buccaneers fight their way back, running the ball right at the Falcon defense. They break them down and are tiring them out. They take back 14 of the 21-point lead by sheer force and desire to win the game. The Falcon defense looks broken and beaten. They need a rest. Mike needs to get the offense on the field and keep them there. The clock ticks down, signaling the end of the third quarter.

When the Falcons go back onto the field they know the drill. Run the ball and keep running the ball. Throw short passes to gain yards and first downs but use the clock. And they do, they use eight minutes driving the ball down the field. They can't get the touchdown but kick a field goal. The lead is now 10. The defense is rested and the lead is increased. Mike has done his job. There are only a few minutes left and they know they can hold them. These minutes seem like hours. They Falcon players on the sideline are holding their heads in their hands for fear of what's about to happen. It is gut wrenching.

The Buccaneers go with a no-huddle offense. They throw quick, short passes, 10 yards at a time. Within two minutes they are within field goal range. The crowd screams. The players on the sidelines work the crowds by jumping up and down with their hands pumping up and down to rev up the crowd.

It is first down and the Buccaneers are on the Falcon's 35. The quarterback goes back to throw, and the blitz is on. He runs out of the pocket, scrambling and looking down field. No one is open. The quarterback doesn't see the lineman coming from behind him, but he feels him slam into him from behind. He wraps his arms around his stomach and shoves his head into the ground. Suddenly the ball is a free agent tumbling to the ground. Everything seems to come to a halt, as if slow motion. The crowd roars and motion slows with every second that it takes the ball to make its way to the ground. The players on the field are in slow motion and when the ball hits the ground, helmets into the turf, bodies colliding, sounds of pain, everything is in real time again

The ball is out and a Falcon is right there to pick it up, but as soon as he does he is slammed into the ground by two large Buccaneers. It doesn't matter. The Falcon's have the ball back with just over two minutes on the clock. All Mike needs to do is wait for the two-minute warning, get one first down and then down the ball four times. The game will be over and they will be victorious.

The Jumbotron pops up image after image of the fans, painted red and gold faces, screaming kids wearing their favorite player's jersey. They are going to the NFC Championship game!

"What a lucky break for the Falcons," says Madden.

"Lucky? I think they had this game won from the start," replies Troy.

"Well now they do for sure, unless they do something crazy."

"They should sit Chambers and let him rest. Bring in the back-up, run the ball a couple of plays and get a first down. Then it's all over."

"You're right, Troy. This game is over."

When the clock ticks down to zero the crowd goes running onto the field. It is just like when Mike was in college. The team is quickly escorted off the field. The energy in the box builds as the wives press their faces against the glass, not allowing one single gaze to leave the field. One more game and their husbands are going to the Super Bowl, most of them for the first time. It's almost unbelievable. After a few moments pass they start to tell Sadie how happy they are Mike played and how they couldn't have done it without him. All the wives and girlfriends wait in the box until the riff-raff clears the stadium and they're free to make their way to the locker room. They will want to celebrate tonight.

The team is greeted by groupies and screaming fans and wives and children and anyone who has every loved the Falcons and wants just a little touch of the success that they've had.

Mike walks out into the madness and he hears someone yell, "Enjoy it while you can Chambers! You're time will come!"

He quickly turns to see who was screaming at him but he doesn't see anything. He continues to push through the crowd of women and men, several pleading for his autograph. One young blond pulls her t-shirt down and exposes her breast, "Mike, can I have your autograph?" She gives him a look like she wants to eat him for dinner. He just pushes past her when he hears the same voice scream out again, "What's wrong Mike, nothing scares you?"

This time Mike stops. He looks over to his right and that's when he sees her. It looks like Sarah but it can't be. Last time he spoke to his mother she said Sarah was still in the hospital. He tries to push through the crowd to get to Sarah but it's no use, there are too many people. Then he feels Ed grab his arm.

"Where you going, man?" Ed asks. He's inviting everyone over to his house for a celebration party.

Ed lives in one of the wealthiest neighborhoods in Atlanta, in a gated community. His house reminds Sadie of his wife, over the top. It's a giant white house with columns in the front. The front doors are huge and very ornate with giant gold handles. You can see the tacky chandelier from the front circular driveway. When you walk in the front doors it's all white imported marble with porcelain statues lined around the circular entrance. The staircase is a grand Cinderella staircase with gold rails. There's a giant painting of Ed and his wife on the wall. They are lying naked on a bearskin rug! Just tacky.

Ed had called ahead to have a caterer come if they won the game, so everything would be ready for them when they arrived. There are food and drinks and even activities for the children. The energy is high at Ed's, the laughter loud, the smiles vast. Nothing can touch this group right now. They won't celebrate too much; they still have two more games to win. While at Ed's, food and drinks are endless.

Mike is the happiest Sadie has ever seen him and for a moment, just a moment, she feels bad about how crappy she treats him. We actually see a human side to her that is warm and not cold. He and his buddies can't stop talking about the game. They all tell Mike they didn't think he could pull it out but he did! Mike loves it. He loves being able to do the impossible.

Sadie sits at a table conversing with a couple of the wives and Mike walks up.

"Hello ladies. How is everyone today?"

"Great Mike, how are you? Great game!"

"Thanks. I am very happy we won," he says as he grabs Sadie's hand and pulls her gently away from the table and away from the crowd. He flirtatiously kisses her and sways side to side to the music in the background. Sadie pushes him away.

"Remember after the championship game in Miami? That was the first time we did it."

"Yeah, I remember."

"Let's do it, right here. No one's watching."

"Mike, we can't."

"Come on Sadie, I feel like I'm in college again. I want you. Maybe tonight we can get pregnant, wouldn't that be perfect!"

Before she could say anything else he kisses her again and forces his hands up her skirt against her silky skin. He rips her panties off and unbuttons his pants. He is inside of her within minutes.

"Stop Mike, I said I don't want to."

"Yeah you do baby, I can feel how wet you are?"

Sadie's body responds but she is uncomfortable. Her body is responding but her mind is not.

"Mike, please, stop it." And then she feels it.

"Thanks honey, I just couldn't wait until we got home to have you. Sorry about your underwear," he chuckles.

She is once again back to the disgust and disdainful feelings Mike brings her to on a daily basis.

"You're a real dick, Mike!" Sadie starts walking off, sorting out her skirt and leaving her torn underwear on the ground.

Mike walks after her, "I never thought I could be this happy. You think we made a baby?"

Sadie stops and quickly turns around. He almost knocks her over.

"I doubt it!" Sadie snips and then turns and walks away.

Mike just stands there, completely surprised by her response.

# Chapter 21

The next morning they are both hung over. Mike climbs out of bed first, moving very slowly. Sadie doesn't move. She is fast asleep.

When he gets to the kitchen he messes around with the cabinets until he finds the toaster. He puts it up on the counter. He gets a glass from the cabinet and fills it with ice from the refrigerator. He grabs the butter out of the refrigerator and walks over to the bread box. Toasts will help absorb the acid that's having a party in his stomach.

He takes his toast and sits on the couch, watching TV for over two hours before Sadie manages to get out of bed. She comes downstairs and goes into the kitchen.

"You didn't make coffee?" she shouts from the kitchen.

"No honey, I'm sorry. I wasn't in the mood for coffee, only water. Do you want me to make you some?"

"No, water's probably a better choice anyway."

She walks into the family room with a large glass of ice water. She puts it down on the table and sits in the chair next to the couch.

"What are you watching?"

"Sports center."

She rolls her eyes.

"So how are you feeling?" Mike asks.

"Hung over. How about you?"

"The same. What a night, huh?"

She looks at Mike, "Yeah, that was fun. I haven't been that..." she pauses, "happy in a long time."

"I know. It was a good night," he smiles. She knows what he's referring to...their little venture out of sight.

"So do you guys have the day off?"

"Yeah, we start back tomorrow. We only have a week but coach wanted to give us a little break. Do you want to do something today?"

"Sure, that would be nice."

"Let's go to the park," offers Mike.

"The park," Sadie looks puzzled. "You want to go to the park!"

"Yes, watch the kids play! Then we can have brunch at that little Italian place on the corner, you know the one."

"Yeah, okay, then we better get dressed."

It's a gorgeous day, the sun is shining but the clouds provide a bit of on-and-off shade. There's a mild breeze you can hear through the trees. Mike is in jeans and a team t-shirt and sneakers. Sadie wears a thin, long, pale blue skirt, so thin the breeze catches it as she walks. She has on a tank top and sandals, with her hair in a ponytail.

When they get to park they sit on the bench and watch the kids play. After they swing they head to the merry-go-round, then the monkey bars and off to the slides. It's like a circuit.

Mike's feels like someone is watching him. He's used to fans following and asking him for his autograph, but this is different. The hairs on the back of his neck are standing on end. He casually looks around, as if he's just taking in his surroundings. He looks to his left, and then slowly to his right. That's when he thinks he sees a short man in a green baseball cap standing behind a tree, watching. Mike doesn't do anything; he just turns his head back. He thinks about what he wants to do—how will he catch this guy without him running away? He decides to get up, pretending to walk over to the trash can. This way he can get a better look at him. As he gets up he looks toward the tree but the man is gone. "Was he even there to begin with?" he wonders. He has been on a lot of medication lately.

They stop off for brunch on the way home. It is 8:00 p.m. when they get back to the house.

"So are you excited for the game?" Sadie asks as they walk into the house.

"Yeah. I'm totally psyched. We can take them no problem. I just hope the defense has a good game. They got beat up pretty badly by Tampa."

"I'm sure it will be fine. How's your knee?"

"It feels good, no problem. I'm surprised. I thought it would be sore today but it's not."

"That's great. Those cortisone shots really work."

"Yes they do," he says as he grabs her and pulls her next to him. "Do you really want to watch TV?" He leans his head down to be next to hers.

"I'm going to watch the news, I need to see if there's anything on about the Peterson trial.

"I'm still a little hung over, I was thinking of going to bed. Do you mind?"

"No honey," she smiles. "I don't mind at all."

"Are you coming up?"

"Yeah, I'll be up in a minute."

"Okay," he says. "Good night."

"Night, honey."

Mike heads upstairs. He goes into the bathroom to brush his teeth. He picks up the tube of paste and it's empty. He can't even roll up the tube and squeeze out enough for one brush. He looks under the sink in the cabinets but there's nothing. He moves over to Sadie's sink and starts shuffling through her cabinets. He can't find any toothpaste. In the back corner of her cabinet is a black velvet box. Curious, he picks it up and takes a look at it. It looks like a generic black velvet covered box, no letters on it, nothing. He opens it up and inside is a place for a perfume bottle. Now he's really curious because he knows he didn't buy the perfume for Sadie.

"Where's the bottle?" He thinks. He's never seen a bottle that shape. He pulls the sleeve out of the box and underneath is a little green plastic box. His temperature starts to rise; he's seen a container like this before in college.

He opens it up and screams, "Sadie!"

A minute later she walks into the bathroom, "What happened, why are you screaming?"

He holds up the green plastic box.

"Oh shit!" She quietly says.

"Oh shit is right Sadie! Birth control pills. Are you fucking kidding me?"

"Look, Mike, we're not married yet and I told you I'm not ready..."

He doesn't let her finish. "Not ready. Sadie, not ready is one thing. Lying to me about being on birth control is another. I can't believe you. I mean, why didn't you just tell me you had absolutely no desire to have a kid? I mean, that would have been better than hiding birth control pills under your sink."

Sadie just stood there quietly, saying nothing.

"You hardly have sex with me and you're on birth control. You're an ass, Sadie." Mike walks into the bedroom, grabs his pillow and leaves the room.

# Chapter 22

The night before the game Mike tosses and turns in the guest bed getting, very little sleep. He is pissed and anxious so his mind switches between envisioning each play and how Sadie lied to him. Mike's mind continues to wander in the land of nod, a smile on his sleeping face and sounds of triumph rumbling through his tired and lifeless lips, almost as if he is snoring words of defeat. He is rudely awakened by the loud buzz of his watch. It is 5:00 a.m. Mike actually feels good; his Super Bowl dreams are not too far away. He gets out of bed and stumbles across the shag carpet, his feet heavy, and his toes tingling because they're still asleep. He shuffles his feet one after the other, his hands scratch his genitalia then up to his head as his heavy eyes slightly open and his mouth breaths a huge yawn and moan in one.

Mike enters his room and walks into the bathroom, drops his drawers and grabs himself to pee. Sadie can hear the water running in the bathroom and she puts a pillow over her head. After washing up, Mike is more alive. He exits the bathroom and makes his way to his closet. Where he tosses on some sweats and a t-shirt, grabs his bag of gear and is off with a whistle.

On his way out of the bedroom he looks at his sleeping wife. A knowing moan filters out from under the covers. He walks out of the room.

The team hovers in the dark, quiet and moldy-smelling locker room to review last weeks' plays. The energy is upbeat but soon to rise when the coach starts to holler and get them pumped up for the game. Then they spend an hour working on the plays for the game. They run some drills and practice a few plays. Lunch is brought in so as to keep them all prisoner in the musty locker room. But they are used to it.

By 12:15 they are dressed and ready to head out to the field for warm-ups. There isn't a minute to spare. By this time the team is pumped up with adrenaline. The music from the field filters through into the locker room. The guys are jazzed. Some do a little jig and dance to really get in the mood to kick some Cowboy ass.

"Let's roll," shouts the coach. A roar of testosterone-filled screams is heard and the team runs to the field. Fireworks burst into the air with a screeching sound and a whistle as they explode while the Falcons hit the field. The announcer introduces the team as the fireworks explode and the crowd roars throughout the stands. A wave is started by one fan-filled section and it rolls throughout the stadium until the Falcons make their way to their side of the field. The crowd is pumped and so is the team. Any nervousness that Mike felt is gone now.

The wind is really kicking up now and the clouds are black. The teams line up on opposite sides of the field for the national anthem. The moment is pivotal and intense. Sarah McLachlan sings. It is bone-chilling. The crowd loves her and screams for her when she is done. The players line up and start their calisthenics and stretches. Mike throws the ball a bit with his quarterback coach, Kevin, to warm up his arm. The fans are piling into the stadium with painted faces, red shirts, hot dogs and beer in hand. Everyone is ready for a battle.

Fights start up between Dallas and Atlanta fans but the players don't even notice. They are focused on the game. Security takes care of the disputes and the players head back into the locker room. In the locker room the coach sits them all down and gives them his motivating speech about the game and winning and playing with heart. At the end they all get up and stand together. Mike, as the leader of the team, starts the final chant.

"Who are we?" He screams.

Everyone yells, "FALCONs"

"I said, who are we?" Mike screams again.

"FALCONs" they scream back.

"And what do we do?"

"We soar and we kill."

"Then let's do it, Falcons!"

A wave is started again as the captains walk to the center of the field for the coin toss. Atlanta wins the toss-up and chooses to kick. Each team takes their place on the field and the ball is in motion, starting the game. The special teams run onto the field. There is no turning back now. The crowd is intense with excitement

Cynthia flew in this morning alone to visit to watch the game. It just seems too exhausting and too important of a game to deal with her daughter, and she and Sadie will have fun together. A lot rides on this game. If they win, there will be a celebration like never before, if they lose there will be an uproar— both scenarios not fit for a kid but absolutely fit for her and Cynthia. Most of the wives are without their children for the very same reasons. Everyone is nervous. A win means private jets to Paris for all. A loss means spending the summer at their own pool with their screaming kids.

When Cynthia and Sadie sit down, the first wife starts in.

"I hope that husband of yours knee is in top shape," says one of the wives.

Sadie gives a nervous look, "I know. I think it is. He's been doing a lot of therapy and seems to be walking fine." Sadie replies.

"Thank God." Another wife chimes in. "It's all riding on him, sweetie" as she lifts her glass of wine as if to give a toast. She is already a little tipsy and it seems she's going for the goal herself!

"No pressure, ladies, Thanks" Sadie replies back in a facetious way.

"Hun, we mean no harm. We're just hoping Mike pulls the team through. We all need to be kept in handbags and shoes!" Everyone chuckles. "I'll drink to that," say a wife before raises her glass again. Everyone laughs, "Here, here" as they clink their glasses.

Sadie and Cynthia sit down in their seats. No one even cares to be introduced to Cynthia.

Cynthia whispers to her, "What's up with these women? Are they like this every game?"

"Every game," says Sadie. "It's always the same shit. It's just like I told you at the party we threw for Mike's parents."

"Well then, let's see who can sling shit the farthest," says Cynthia. They both laugh.

The first quarter is a blur. Second quarter starts with the coach pacing up and down the sideline, verbally abusing Mike as if everything is riding on him. Mike tries to ignore him but he still needs to listen to the plays. The entire quarter is a bust but there is nothing he can do. They have every man covered and sometimes double covered. The defense is performing well but they can't keep this pace up all game. Mike must step up and work on a different game plan.

The team is fumbling all over the field. The coach calls a time out. Kevin, the quarterback coach, corners Mike on the sideline during the break between quarters.

"Mike, I want to show you a couple new plays. I have some new ideas." He says excitedly.

"All right coach, but don't you think it's risky to make play changes mid game?" Mike pants. He's still recovering from the last series of plays.

"No, not at all. You can do this. They aren't that complicated." He says as he holds up his play book and shows it to Mike.

They review several play options. The entire offense huddles to hear the new plan of attack. The team breaks and are pumped for their new play.

Within 60 seconds they score. Mike demonstrates four almost perfect spiral long passes down the field and they're in the end zone. It is beautiful. Now the real game has actually begun. This is the turning point. By the end of the 2$^{nd}$ quarter the Falcons lead the Cowboys by 14 points. Half time approaches and the teams run to their respective locker rooms. The crowd chants, "Go Falcons!" The song "Stronger" is heard throughout the stadium. The players are pumped and ready for more.

Sadie and Cynthia leave the box for half time. Sadie has on jeans, a Falcons jersey and sneakers today so she's hard to catch. Cynthia is in black pants and a yellow short sleeved top with red ribbon threaded through the center, under the breasts. Sadie thinks, "Cynthia always knew how to dress for attention."

They walk out into the stands to see the half-time show. The Falcons held a state-wide competition to decide which band would play. It is a huge opportunity for an up-and-coming band. The band marches victoriously onto the field. Their genre of music is '70s disco so one can imagine the commotion on the field and in the stands. The band members are clad in green-and-white polyester outfits and don rainbow wigs as a bit of fancy flair. The outfits are a perfect complement to the rainbow flags that the twirlers whip in the wind. As the band takes its place in the middle of the field the crowd boosts from their seats in a frenzy of dance and hysteria. During the middle of the set Kenny Chesney walks onto the field and the crowd roars with disbelief and excitement. And suddenly a rush of 1,000 screaming fans comes running onto the field. They surround Kenny and his band as they sway to his hit song, "In a Small Town." The crowd loves it! At the end of the set a huge firework ensemble shoots into the now darkened sky, delivering an amazing encore setup for one final song. Kenny sings one of his most notable tunes, "She Thinks My Tractor's Sexy," and the half-time show is proved to be a huge success.

The crowd loves it! Cynthia and Sadie are dancing in the aisle. The huge fireworks show actually looks nice against the black sky.

After the band exits the field, the announcers come on the intercom and tell what they believe to be witty jokes about the first half of the game. This repartee is met with a numb reception from the crowd. Both teams rush the field and the crowd stands up in a moment of pumped-up testosterone-infused energy as they scream and moan and clap and throw things and whistle and jump up and down. The game is back on. Oh yeah!

Soon the teams are back onto the field to start the second half. The Falcons look ready. The Falcons are ready. Their performance is on fire as they mirror the second quarter and bring their team ahead by 21 points. Mike and Ed are in the zone and no one can touch them. The Cowboy's defense has exhausted themselves from running up and down the field and being pummeled in one play after another. The Falcons are red hot and the fans are in a complete state of hysteria. Chants abound throughout the stadium, pumping the Falcons more and putting a damper on the Cowboys. You can see the Cowboy frustration on the sidelines as the coach paces up and down the sidelines yelling at the players. The players sit on the bench with towels over their heads, beaten and broken. The Cowboy fans are silent!

Ed and Mike have played so well they are near record-breaking points. The announcers add pressure by making this announcement but the guys are so pumped that they don't even hear what's going on outside of their minds repeatedly telling them they are kicking ass and are the best at what they do.

"These guys are hot today Troy, it's like they're in the zone." Madden states.

"You know, it's a wonderful feeling when you have that perfect timing with your receiver. It's harmonious."

"Did you say harmonious?" Madden chuckles. "Getting in touch with your intelligent side, Troy?"

"What's wrong, John. That word too big for you? Too many syllables?" Troy quips."

"Yeah, that's it. Well Mr. Harmonious, what do you think of the Cowboy's defense today—pretty weak, huh?"

"Well, they're certainly not playing like they should."

"Embarrassed to call yourself a Cowboy today, huh Troy?" Madden laughs.

"Look, they have a great team but they haven't decided to come play the game. Every team has bad games; you just hope they're not during the Divisional Championship."

"You got that right!" Madden just laughs. He loves razing Troy.

The Falcons go on to put up 14 more points in the 4th quarter. Ed has a record game, scoring 28 points in the 2nd half. Mike is 26 of 35 for the game. No one expects this kind of point spread—they were looking for more like 7 to 10 points in the Cowboy's favor. Mike and Ed want the win more than anyone can imagine and they go out on the field and take it. The 4th quarter is coming to an end and the clock ticks down from 10 seconds. The crowd counts along and when it hit zero, they go nuts.

It has been years since Atlanta has won a division championship game and the fans go crazy. The teams rush off the field quickly before the fans mob them. It is an amazing time but it's scary to think of having fans rush. Most are so inebriated they wouldn't feel a thing if they were hurt. Thank God for pads on the players.

There is one screaming crazy fan after the other scaling the yellow end-field goal posts. And before you know it, there are fans covering the entire goal. The goals shake so badly one would think they would come down. It takes over an hour to get these diehard fans off the field. It is a mass hysteria on the field. Up in the box the women see what's going on.

"Look at those fools" says Jessica as she sways and slurs her words and gives a good drunken giggle.

"Hey, those fools keep our husbands earning the big bucks my dear," Gail says in her ear.

"Ha," the drunk wails out, "I'll..." and as she says, "drink to that" they all chime in. Everyone laughs.

Sadie and Cynthia make a quick exit through the underground pathway. Sadie doesn't wait for Mike as usual. Her insensitivity towards Mike's victory rings through loudly as all she can muster up in her cold mind is a text message letting him know she is leaving for home.

The locker room is loud—lockers banging, men jumping up and doing chest nudges, showers running, screaming, muscles flaring, sweat pouring off as water and soap hit the skin and wash off the stench. It is an amazing room to be in. The energy is intense. Mike chats to Ed about how good he played and a beep is heard. He picks up his phone. It is a text from Sadie.

Mike's buddy, "Sadie bail again?"

"Yeah, man." He thinks back to last night and the birth control pills. "She's just not that into partying. But I am!" Mike screams with excitement. "Fuck her" Mike says.

"Yeah man, let's partayyyyy," says Ed.

This is a big night for them. It's a big night for Atlanta. They have worked hard to get to the championship and winning is the highlight of their careers, their lives at this moment. Nothing could be better.

When Sadie and Cynthia get home they are a bit tipsy from the game. They sit in the family room drinking and playing backgammon. They put Matchbox 20 and sing all the words. This was always an old college favorite.

At 3:30 am Mike stumbles into the house with the scent of perfume on him and not a care in the world. He and his boys had the time of their lives and he didn't need Sadie with him. It was actually more fun without her.

Cynthia wakes up when she hears Mike come in. She listens for an argument or some activity but hears nothing. She goes back to sleep.

# Chapter 23

The next morning Sadie wakes up to find Mike passed out next to her. She makes a lot of noise as she leaves the room, just to make sure he doesn't get too good of a sleep. Sadie is just about to butter a piece of toast when Mike walks into the kitchen.

"What are you doing up? I thought you would sleep until at least noon?" Sadie says sarcastically.

"No, I feel good. That is enough sleep for one night," he says as he walks over to the coffee pot. He stares at the coffee pot. His stomach is sending him strong messages and wanting coffee is not one of them. He walks away.

Cynthia walks into the kitchen. You could cut the tension with a knife.

"Morning. Great game yesterday, Mike."

"Thanks, Cynthia." He says and doesn't even look up.

Sadie starts to makes Cynthia a cup of coffee. They sit down at the bar and have coffee together.

"So, what are you going to do today, Mike?" Sadie whispers under her breadth, "If you can do anything at all after what you must have done last night."

"I don't know, what do you guys want to do?"

"I have to run some errands, and then drop Cynthia off at the airport."

"Yeah, what errands?" Mike snips.

"You know, groceries, stop off at work to drop off some papers, go by the bank, nothing exciting."

"Well, I think I'll just hang around here. Coach sent me home with some tapes to watch and some plays to look over. How long will you be gone?"

"Why, you planning on having a party?"

"Funny Sadie, really funny."

"Not long, a few hours."

"I'll see you when you get home then. Have a safe flight, Cynthia."

"Thanks, Mike. Good luck in the Super Bowl."

"Thanks."

"Well, let's go upstairs and get dressed." Sadie says.

"Okay."

They go upstairs, and get dressed. Cynthia is up, packed and showered. They load her bags into the car and head out for the morning.

Cynthia's never been a fan of Mike's so a one-night stay is perfect for her. Sadie gets home around 2:00 p.m. and Mike is asleep on the couch. The TV is playing a video of the game and a cup of coffee from this morning is on the table in front of him. He is still in the clothes they left him in. She doesn't want to wake Mike and have to deal with him so she goes out to the car to get the groceries.

She brings the bags in from the car. As she is putting away the groceries she looks into the family room to see if Mike is still asleep. He hasn't moved. She finishes putting away the groceries and then sits down to go through some papers. About 20 minutes later she gets up to go into the family room and turns off the TV. She doesn't care much for football so listening to it play on TV is a bit annoying. She turns the TV it off and notices Mike still hasn't moved. She walks over to the couch to take a closer look. She notices his mouth is open and has some white stuff in the corner and it seems to be dripping down his face. This doesn't look like drool but something else. She nudges him a bit.

"Mike, wake up. We're home." She sort of kicks him but she really could care less if he moves or not. He was out all night!

Mike's head falls to the side and that's when she sees it. There is blood all over the back of his head. As she is looking at the wound to try to figure out what happened, a woman comes out from the bathroom across the room. Sadie gasps and falls back onto her backside on the floor. She hits her spine on the coffee table. The woman walks up to her very slowly, just looking at her like she's burning Sadie's image into her brain.

"Who are you?" Sadie asks in a quivering voice.

The woman just stares at her, getting closer. She has a gun in her right hand, dangling at her side.

"What do you want?" Sadie is starting to sob a bit. "What do you want," she screams.

"He didn't belong to you," Sarah says as she stands directly behind the couch, looking down at Mike's dead body. "He was mine. He was always mine." She slowly takes her glance off of Mike and moves it to Sadie.

"What are you talking about?" Sadie cries. "Who are you?"

"I'm the one who really loved him," she snips. "Not you! Not you!" Her eyes are wild and she's looking at Sadie as if she had just seen Satan himself.

Sadie gets up and tries to run for the front door but Sarah grabs her by the arm and throws her down to the ground.

"You never loved him like I did," Sarah says in a child-like voice. She turns to look back at Mike lying on the couch. "I loved him from the moment I saw him." She smiles.

"What do you want from me?" Sadie cries.

Sarah turns back to Sadie, "What do you mean? Why would I want something from you? You are nothing to me." Sarah walks back to the couch, gun still in hand, and looks down at Mike. She bends down and kisses him on the forehead. "I love you, my darling," she whispers. Slowly she stands back up, lifting the gun in her hand. It's now pointed at Sadie. Sadie is quivering on the floor. Sarah brings the gun up closer to her head, right under her chin and pulls the trigger. The back side of her head blows open and pieces spread from the couch behind her to the wall. Sadie screams!

It takes her a few minutes to compose herself enough to get up, walk past the body and go into the kitchen to call the police. She sits down in a chair at the bar, staring out into the room with no real view of anything. Within minutes police and an ambulance are at the house. Sadie hears the sirens but doesn't move. The garage door is still open from when she came home. A policeman comes through the garage door, looks around the kitchen and sees Sadie sitting at the bar.

"Are you okay, is everything okay?"

Sadie doesn't respond. The policeman moves into the family room where he sees and examines the two bodies. He goes to the front door and unlocks it. A few more policemen and the EMT crew rush in through the front door in their pressed uniforms. The EMT crew has their hands full of equipment and a gurney.

"Where is he," one asks?

"He's through here," the first on the scene policeman responds.

They get to the couch and immediately start checking out Mike's body, and taking photographs. His lips are blue and drool is hanging from his lower lip. The EMT guys are staring down at him in complete disbelief. They couldn't save the quarterback of the Atlanta Falcons.

A crowd of neighbors are congregating in her front yard, waiting to see what's happening. No one approaches the house. The paramedics put Mike on the gurney, cover his body and face, and roll him out of the house into the ambulance. Behind Mike is a second gurney with Sarah's body on it. When the EMT guys exit the house with a covered body on the gurney, their question is answered. It's Mike Chambers, and he's dead.

The telephone rings. Sadie hears it and her automatic reaction is to answer it. It's the coach calling to check in on Mike.

"Hey Sadie, how are you," he asks?

Sadie doesn't respond.

"Sadie, you there? Everything okay?"

The other end of the line is silent.

"Sadie, what's going on?" The coach's voice is more forceful now. It wakes Sadie up.

"I don't know." And she hangs up.

At this point Sadie is sitting in a chair with her face in her hands. She doesn't cry but just sits there.

# Chapter 24

The rays from the sun shine through the break in the curtains, filling the room with beams of light. Sadie sleeps but the light peeking through the curtains and the songs of the birds wake her. She covers her face with the pillow but it doesn't help. A soft and irritated sigh rings through the room as Sadie contemplates getting out of bed. One leg hangs off the side as the other one slowly makes it way to join its partner. Sadie slides out of the bed; her feet land softly on the wood floor. She creeps to the curtains that so rudely woke her up and pulls them closed so as to block the sun completely. A point that is moot as she is already awake and out of bed. Sadie looks lovingly at her bed as if she were about to crawl back in but realizes it's 6:10 in the morning and probably best for her to start her day, as grueling as she knows it will be. She must brave the storm of Mike's death.

The doorbell rings. Sadie is startled. Who would be at the house at 6:00 in the morning? Sadie puts on her robe and heads down the staircase and to the front door. The house is a mess. Clothes, dishes, books, flowers are everywhere and in no particular order. Sadie hired the cleaning staff she started using after Mike's parents' party but told them not to come the day before. She wanted to be alone—no disturbances. Sadie peeks through the eye hole in the door. It is Mike's parents. They weren't supposed to be here until noon. Sadie takes a big breath in to relax herself. She just saw them at Christmas but it's always uncomfortable when they are around.

"Hang on a minute," says Sadie as she unlatches the brass locks on the door. Before she opens the door, she makes certain her robe is closed properly and she hand-brushes her tousled hair. Sadie swings open the door. "Bob, Susan, hello. I'm so sorry; I had no idea you were coming this early. "Come in, come in. Please." Bob leans in and embraces Sadie so tightly it cuts off her breath. Sobs pour out of Bob's sad face and Susan follows suit. Sadie stands there, unable to breathe. Mike's parents are uncontrollable.

"Oh my. Oh my. I'm so sorry" says Sadie. "Come in."

"We're so sorry darling; we don't know how to describe... My boy, my boy! How did this happen?" says Bob.

"Come in, sit down, please. Over here." Sadie motions to the sofa in the front sitting room.

"How was the drive?" Sadie asks in a weak attempt to calm them down.

Susan looks old and pale, as if a surgeon had never touched her face; her age came through overnight. It truly saddens Sadie to see them this way and she empathizes as she knows loss all too well.

Once the tears stopped flowing like Niagara Falls, Bob answers,

"The drive was fine. How are you holding up, Sadie?"

"Okay. I forgot I took the phone off the hook. The media keeps calling and I've sent the cleaning crew away so I could be alone."

"No wonder you were surprised to see us. They were here when Bob called—Joyce, right Bob? He told them we would be here early."

"So what happened Sadie?" Bob asks again. "They took both bodies to the hospital. Has the coroner prepared the body so we can take him home?"

"Not yet. I'm waiting to hear from him today, actually. It seems unbelievable, I know, but they just don't know what happened yet." Sadie gets up to deflect the conversation.

"Would you like some coffee? I can make a pot."

Wiping the tears from her eyes with a tissue, "That would be lovely, dear. It was a long road, as you can imagine!" says Susan.

"Absolutely. Absolutely." Sadie walks around the corner into the kitchen and calls Bob and Susan, "In here. We can sit at the breakfast table. It will be more comfortable,"

"Here Susan, sit here, and Bob, you over here." Sadie pulls the chairs out for them at the table. "Sorry it's such a mess."

"Oh dear, please. We understand completely" says Bob.

"Thanks Bob." Sadie clutches her robe at her chest, realizing that she's very inappropriately dressed.

"Oh, my, look at me. Will you excuse me for a second so I can go change my clothes?"

"Never mind us," says Bob.

"Certainly dear, that's probably a good idea" says Susan as she glares at her husband. "We will wait right here." Susan says.

"Um, the sugar is next to the microwave and there's also sweetener, Mike always liked sweetener." Sadie breaks down and cries. She puts her hands over her red face and swollen eyes so as to hide her emotional outburst. Susan gets up from her chair and hugs Sadie. She is crying, too.

"There, there. We loved our Mikey. Don't cry. You're making me cry again, too, and just when I had found a decent break!"

Sadie wipes her eyes and finds a giggle deep within her gut, "You're right. I'm sorry. I'll be right back."

"Sure, Sure. Take your time, dear" says Susan.

Sadie goes to the bedroom. Susan makes Bob a cup of coffee and sits at the table.

"I think she's still in shock" says Bob.

"Bob, we're all in shock. Our boy is dead." Susan breaks down again.

"Hunny, we will get through this. Mike would want us to get through this. Be tough. That's what he always told us." Bob leans in and gives his wife a very gentle and loving pat on her arm. "I love you hunny. We will make it through this. I promise" says Bob.

"I know we will, darling, I just don't want to. Why do we have to? I cannot believe."

"Okay, stop it, darling. Let's just drink our coffee" says Bob.

When Sadie comes back down she's in jeans and a white t-shirt. She pours herself a cup of coffee and sits at the table, looking out the back window. Fifteen minutes pass and Bob is back in the kitchen with Sadie.

"I'm sorry Sadie, but I just don't understand. I don't want Susan to hear us talk, either. It's too upsetting for her. I know you said you came home and he was on the couch, but I just don't understand. How did she get into the house? You didn't see a car out front, nothing. No one heard the gunshots?" Bob's voice is full of pain, urgency and distress.

"I don't think so, Bob, but I really wouldn't know. When I walked in I came in through the garage and wasn't't really looking outside for cars. I have no idea when she shot him or why."

"I just can't believe it."

"I can't either. I mean, it just seems surreal. I would have never imagined this happening to Mike," Sadie said with such honesty in her voice.

"To Mike," Bob questions? "This happened to more than Mike, Sadie. What about you and us?"

Sadie, slightly startled, says, "Of course, Bob, of course. I just mean, it's hard to believe someone would shoot him."

Sadie looked at Bob with a little fear in her eyes.

Just as Sadie finishes her statement, Susan came in the kitchen. As Bob walks out the back door behind Susan he asks, "So when will the coroner be finished with Mike, Sadie?

"I think sometime around 3:00," he says. I'm not really sure."

"Is he going to call?"

"Yes. He should call as soon as he's ready. Then he'll release the body so we can get him ready to transport. Is everything ready for him in Blytheville?"

"Can't we go and see the body?"

"Sure, if you want to Bob. I wouldn't recommend it. It's only going to upset Susan. Why don't we wait until we get him back to Blytheville and the mortuary has had some time with his body?"

"We'll see. I'll talk to Susan and see what she wants to do." Bob walks through the door and shuts it behind him.

The phone rings and Sadie answers. It is Mike's sister. She is taking care of all of the arrangements at the funeral home and with the transport from Atlanta to Blytheville.

"Hello," answers Sadie.

"Hi Sadie, it's Michelle," she says abruptly. Michelle and Sadie have never been friends, and rarely speak to each other. Sadie hasn't seen Michelle since college graduation. "I've just spoken to Blytheville Mortuary and they have made all the arrangements for Mike. Are you going to be bringing him back today?"

"Yes. I spoke with Mike's best friend Ed yesterday and took care of everything."

"Good. They're going to have everything set up for the viewing tomorrow. The funeral will be on Thursday. Did my mom and dad get there okay?"

"Yes, they did. They're out back now. Do you want to speak to them?"

"No. I have too much to do planning everything for Mike's funeral," she snaps. Sadie knows she is angry but she doesn't want to deal with her and fighting over the plans for the funeral. It is better to just let Michelle do it all herself.

"I really appreciate all of your help, Michelle. You don't know how much it..." before Sadie could finish Michelle hung up.

Bob and Susan come back in.

"Was that the coroner on the phone, Sadie?" Bob asks eagerly. "Is Mike's body ready?"

"No, no Bob. It was Michelle. She's made all the arrangements for Mike." Sadie looks at both of them, "I'm sorry I'm not doing more."

"You're sorry. I feel so bad for you, for what you saw. Don't worry about Michelle." Susan cries.

The phone rings again and Sadie answers, "Hello."

"I've been trying to call for the last hour, is everything okay?" Ed asks.

"Yes, everything's fine."

"Some of the players wanted to come by the house today—will that be okay."

"Honestly Ed, I don't mind if you come by but I'm not really in the mood for a lot of people."

"No worries, Sadie. I understand. I'll let them know and tell them maybe later."

"Thanks Ed."

"How are you holding up?"

"Good. We're good. Mike's parents are here now, which is great." It's a struggle for Sadie to get the words out. "We're going to get everything ready to take Mike back home today."

"Okay, well, if you need anything we're here."

"Thanks Ed, really. I'm okay."

"All right, then we'll see you at the funeral. Do you have the details yet?"

"Mike's sister just called me and she's going to be letting you know later this morning. Hopefully you can pass it around to everyone."

"No problem. I'll take care of it."

"Talk to you later, Ed."

"Bye, Sadie."

Sadie hangs the phone up. The phone rings again.

"Now you see why I took it off the hook," Sadie says as she starts to get up.

"Let me take care of it, Sadie. You go do what you need to do."

Bob answers the phone, and yells to Sadie.

241

"Sadie, some man named Dan from New York is on the phone. He says you should remember him; he talked to Mike a little while back. He's the friend of John's."

Sadie stops dead in her tracks. Her heart beats faster. Dan, she thinks, Dan. The reporter guy who thought John and Cyrus were connected? She tells Bob she'll take it upstairs.

"Hello, Sadie is that you?" Dan says eagerly.

"Yes, Dan, it's me. It's been a long time." Sadie's voice is soft and a bit broken.

"When I heard the news about Mike and I had to call. I'm so sorry."

"Thank you Dan. That's very nice."

"Well, I have to tell you, I'm not completely surprised. Are you?"

"I don't understand what you mean."

"First Cyrus, then John and now Mike? They're all dead."

"I don't understand? What do you mean, Dan?"

"Maybe it's just the reporter in me Sadie, but there has to be a connection. I mean come on, three best friends all in similar circumstances."

"I don't see how you can say that, Dan," Sadie's voice is very curt now. "Mike's dead. Last time I checked Cyrus and John were alive and Mike was shot to death by some stalker."

"Again, I'm sorry. I don't mean to be rude."

Sadie interrupts him, "Well, you are being rude. I don't care what you think, or what you want to think Mr. Seagirt. Mike's dead and there's nothing you or I can do about it. Now leave me alone." Sadie hangs up. She doesn't want to hear from Dan again!

Sadie comes back downstairs and goes into the kitchen.

"I need to go out for a bit; can you guys manage?"

"Sure, but where are you going? Who was that man on the phone? You seem upset Sadie," Bob asks.

"It's nothing, Bob, just a reporter trying to see if I will talk to him about that crazy woman who shot Mike."

"Okay, but I don't see why that would upset you so much."

"I'm not upset," Sadie snaps.

"Okay, okay sweetie, just calm down," says Susan.

"I'm sorry. I'm tired and upset and I need to go take care of some paperwork and to the hospital and see what they found out about Mike." Sadie grabs her keys and purse and is out the door.

A few hours later, she is heading back home. As she approaches the house she sees the line of cars parked at her house. There must be 15 people at her house. She drives up the drive but the press is everywhere and she can't get into her garage.

She's getting frustrated, covering her face when she hears Bob. He is screaming at the photographers and pushing them out of the way so Sadie can park. She parks her car in the garage. Bob keeps the photographers from entering the garage. When Sadie closes the garage door her father goes inside through the front door. She sits in her car, not wanting to go inside. She gets ready to open her car door when Bob opens the door to the house. He sees her sitting in the car. He walks down the stairs and to her side of the car. She opens the door and gets out.

"Everything okay Sadie? Those photographers are crazy."

"Everything's fine, Bob. I just saw all the cameras and didn't know what to do. Who's in the house? I don't know if I feel like seeing anyone right now."

"I know, honey, its okay. No one expects you to want to entertain. They just want to show you that they're here for you and try to help if they can."

"I know. I'm just tired. The reporters attacked me at the coroners and I had to fight to get to my car, then here at my house. They just won't leave me alone!"

Bob gives Sadie a big hug. "It's going to be okay, Sadie. It's just gonna take a little time. It will all calm down, you'll see."

"Well, let's go inside. I don't want everyone to think I'm avoiding them."

"That's a girl."

They walk into the house. There are people in the kitchen, on the patio out back, in the family room. It seems like there are people everywhere.

Sadie heads upstairs to calm down. She lies down and falls asleep. Almost three hours go by before Sadie comes back downstairs. Everyone is gone. Susan and Bob are exhausted. Many of the visitors brought food so Sadie sets the table for the three of them to eat. No one is very hungry but they do their best to enjoy the meal. They talk a little. Bob remembers Sadie received a call while she was out.

"Sadie, I almost forgot. Some reporter called the house while you were upstairs. He said you knew him…Dan? He left a number for you to call him back."

As Bob gets up to get her the number, she snaps. "I don't need his number."

"Okay, it's no big deal. I just thought you might want to know he called."

"I'm sorry Bob. I just don't want to talk to him. He keeps calling me every day. I have no idea who he is. Just leave his number on the counter."

Sadie cleans up the guest room for Mike's parents and then goes into her room. She runs a hot bath and sinks down into the water, where she stays for an hour. When she gets out of the bath she crawls into bed and thinks about the day ahead of her. The next two days will be two of the longest days in her life.

# Chapter 25

Sadie wakes up at 7:00 a.m.; she can't believe how late she slept. She has several things to take care of before they leave and now she only has a couple of hours to get them done. She puts on her robe and runs down the stairs into the kitchen. Susan and Bob are having breakfast.

"Good morning, Sadie, we thought we would let you sleep a bit late this morning," Susan says. "Do you want some breakfast?"

"No thanks, Susan. I'll just grab a cup of coffee. I have a few things I need to get done before we leave."

Sadie makes herself a cup of coffee and then goes upstairs to get ready. Once she is dressed she sits down on the bed to make a few phone calls. The last is to the morgue to make sure the body is ready for transport. They confirm that everything is ready to go. The transport car will be to the hospital this morning to pick up Mike's body and drive him to the funeral home in Blytheville. She hangs the phone up, grabs her coffee and heads downstairs to the kitchen.

"Well, everything's ready." Sadie says quietly.

"That's good, Sadie. Why don't you sit and have some breakfast? You didn't eat any dinner and it's going to be a long day," Susan says.

"I'm not really hungry, Susan. But I'll have a piece of toast if it will make you feel better."

"It will, thank you."

Susan butters a piece of toast for Sadie and hands it to her on a plate.

"What else do you need to do before we leave?" Bob asks/

"Just pack. It shouldn't take me too long."

"Okay, I'll start loading up the car. You can bring your bag down when you're ready. I'll put it in your car for you."

Sadie finishes her toast and heads upstairs to pack. By 10:00 am they are on the road to Blytheville. Susan made little snack bags for her and Sadie for the drive. Sadie follows them out of Atlanta.

They are about 30 minutes into the drive when Cynthia calls Sadie.

"Hello Sweetie, how are you?"

"I'm good, I'm driving to Blytheville."

"Good? I doubt you're good. I'll be there soon, sweetie."

"I know. I can't wait to see you. Things have been crazy and I can't get that girl's face out of my head."

"I hate to say it now but you're going to need a bit of therapy, Sadie."

"Great, can't wait for that, Cyn."

"It will be good for you. You have a few things that I think would be good for you to deal with. But we can talk about that later. I'll call you when I land. Bye, sweetie."

"Bye, Cyn."

She doesn't see the Taurus.

They arrive at Mike's house at around 2:30 and drop Sadie and Susan off. The house is a two-story colonial, red brick with four large white columns in the front. The shutters on the windows are white as well. There is a drive along the side of the house and a circular drive in front with beautiful flowers along the asphalt. The drive along the side has a two-car garage at the end with a small apartment on top. It's designed to look exactly like the house in red brick. Sadie always thought Mike tried to copy his parents' home with his own.

Bob drives to the funeral home to make sure everything is ready. Mike's body should have arrived. The viewing is supposed to begin in a few hours. Bob needs to meet Michelle and finish the funeral preparations for tomorrow and make sure that the day will go just as they want. The girls will join them for the viewing at 6:00; this way they won't have to stay there a long time. It is a draining experience and most people just want to say good bye to Mike.

They get back to the house around 8:00 pm and Susan goes into the kitchen to warm up some food neighbors have dropped off. Sadie isn't very hungry. She finishes eating, has a bath, and then goes to bed in Mike's old room. They haven't changed a thing since Mike left. There is a double bed with a football duvet cover. They bordered the room with the flags of all of the professional football teams. In the center of the room is a Bama circle rug. There are two large windows on one wall, a closet on the other. In between the two windows is a desk with a wood chair. There are photos and pictures on the desk as well as papers. Next to the closet is a dresser with a TV sitting on top. The TV looks so old it must have vacuum tubes inside.

Sadie takes a shower and then goes into Mike's old room to go to bed. She wanders around the room, imagining Mike's life as a child, going through his pictures and drawers, looking at his childhood memories.

Sadie climbs into bed and stares at the ceiling until she falls asleep. It seems like she just puts her head on the pillow when Susan is telling her to come down for breakfast.

"Get up. It's time for breakfast."

"Okay Susan, just give me a minute."

"Okay but we have a lot to do today."

"Okay, just a minute."

Sadie looks over at the clock; it is 7:15 a.m. She rolls out of bed and puts on some jeans and a shirt. She walks downstairs and into the kitchen, Susan is pouring her a cup of coffee.

"Good morning. I've made you some coffee, just like you like it."

"Thanks, Susan," Sadie says, starring at Susan with a look of awe. They are burying her son today and she is making coffee. How odd!

Bob and Michelle are running around getting everything ready, probably their way of dealing with the stress. The phone is ringing all morning and the cameras crews are out in full force. Sadie takes her coffee and goes upstairs to get ready. Cynthia arrives at the Chambers house a couple hours before the services begin. She helps Sadie with anything else she needs.

They get dressed, the women in black dresses and Bob in a black suit. Susan, Bob, Sadie and Cynthia get into the limousine waiting outside the house. They are followed by a limousine with Michelle and her family.

It's a beautiful sunny day, clear skies with a slight breeze. It's unusually warm for a winter day. They are driven to the church where Mike had his communion. It's a little white church with a steeple. There are two stained glass windows on either side of the church and oak wood benches. The carpet down the center aisle is dirty and old. There are flowers lined up in the front of the church around the coffin. Mike's coffin is placed at the base of the podium in the front of the church. It is an open casket service. The casket is made of mahogany wood with brushed brass handles. The inside lining is Falcon red with a white pillow placed under Mike's head. He's in a beautiful custom-made grey tuxedo and red button-up shirt. His hair is brushed and sprayed in place; the makeup artist did a wonderful job bringing color back to his face. He looks very peaceful and almost happy.

The service is attended by everyone in Blytheville as well as all of the players, coaches and several reporters. Kids are running up to the players and asking for their autograph; they don't know any better. This is a very small town.

The service is nice; the priest speaks about Mike as a child. Several of his teachers from high school speak and a few of his teammates. The church is full of flowers of all types. People sent flowers from all over the country. There are banners as if the Falcons had won the Super Bowl. They put his team flag over the casket. The service isn't too long; about one hour and they are off to the gravesite. Mike's teammates, led by Ed, carry the casket out of the funeral home into the car.

When they get to the gravesite there are more reporters and more flowers. The gravesite is completely covered with the most beautiful colors, flowers everywhere. The breeze has picked up and it's much cooler now. The trees in the cemetery are bare and brown, the grass is dead. Reporters ran toward the limousine when Sadie arrives, cameras flashing. Sadie and Susan cover their faces while Bob yells to give the women some peace. At least for one day. The Falcon players carry Mike's casket to the gravesite and set it down on the ground. Their faces are solemn.

Susan breaks down when the priest talks about burying Mike and how he is going to join God in heaven.

She starts weeping, "Not my son, why my son?" It upsets everyone to watch her grief. Michelle carries her away to the car so she can sit and grieve alone. The service is short and ends shortly after Michelle and Susan leave. Everyone takes their turn putting a flower on the casket. Cynthia walks to the grave with Sadie. She waits for a couple of minutes and then heads back to the limo alone. Sadie stands by the gravesite for 10 minutes after everyone finishes. Sadie finally puts her flower on the casket and walks back to the car.

On her walk back she notices someone watching behind a tree. It's a man but she can't see him well enough to tell if she knows him. Mike was a famous quarterback; it's probably some fan who didn't want to get too close to the service out of respect. Sadie brushes it off. They drive back to Mike's house.

When they get back to the house most people have already arrived. They are mingling around the house and outside. There is a lot of food and family and friends. Everyone takes the opportunity to come up to Sadie and tell her how sorry they are. They first have to introduce themselves. She meets his elementary and high school teachers. She meets women who say they used to date Mike. She meets lots of people who tell her they are all really good friends of Mike's. Everyone has a story to tell about Mike. Everyone asks Sadie what happened, and tell her they can't believe it. Mike was so young; in the prime of his life.

Sadie thinks if she hears someone say, "I just can't believe it but you know, only God knows when our time is up, and when it's up, it's up," she will scream.

The players have to leave right after the service; they have to get to the game. They all promise Sadie they will win for Mike and bring her the Super Bowl ring!

The day seems to go on forever. It is 8:00 p.m. before the final family members leave. Susan goes to her room an hour after they return to the house from the cemetery and doesn't come out. Bob, Michelle and Cynthia take care of everything around the house. Sadie convinces them to hire a service to take care of everyone and clean up but Bob wants to help. He doesn't want Susan to wake up in the morning and not be able to find anything. Sadie grabs a bottle of wine and a glass and goes out back with Cynthia. Sadie and Cynthia finish the entire bottle of wine, remembering Mike in college.

It is 10:00 am before Sadie wakes up the next morning. She must have passed out from all of the wine because she doesn't remember moving all night. When she tries to move, her head throbs. She desperately wants a glass of water. She manages to get herself out of bed and dresses in sweats so she can go get a drink of water and an aspirin.

When she walks downstairs into the kitchen no one is there. She takes a glass out of the cabinet and goes to the refrigerator for some ice. She sees a note sticking on the refrigerator. She reads it as she walks over to get some water.

> *Sadie, we ran out to drop Cynthia off at*
>
> *the airport and get something*
>
> *to eat. You need your*
>
> *rest so we didn't want to wake you.*
>
> *Be back soon!*

She is honestly relieved to be in the house by herself. She can relax and manage her hangover before they get back home. She grabs some aspirin and her water from the night stand and goes into the family room to watch TV. She hears her cell phone buzzing in her bag. It's a text from Cynthia telling her she'll call her later. She starts to think about the service and then the man behind the tree pops into her head. She wonders if it was Dan. He's tried to call her again since she hung up on him. She doesn't care—so what if he came to the funeral? If he keeps bothering her she'll file a restraining order.

She hears Susan outside the house and knows her time of peace is over. The thought makes her head hurt.

"Hi Sadie, how are you feeling?" Bob says as they walk into the family room where Sadie is sitting on the couch.

"I'm good Bob, thanks."

"You know Sadie; you are welcome to stay as long as you want. There's no rush for you to get back," Bob says as he pats her on the shoulder.

"I know Bob, and thank you. I really just want to get home and spend some time by myself. It's been a really long week."

"Yes, it has. We understand." Bob walks off into the kitchen.

Sadie lounges on the couch for another 30 minutes watching TV, or at least appearing to watch TV. She really can't wait to leave. She wants to get home, with no one around. When she gets enough energy she walks upstairs to pack her bag. By 2:30 she is ready to head back to Atlanta. She needs to get back and pack up her things. Of course she can stay in Mike's house as long as she wants, but that's not what she wants to do.

Bob and Susan stand outside the house waving as Sadie drives off. Susan tucks her head into Bob's shoulder and cries as she drives off.

While driving she receives several text messages from Cynthia but she doesn't respond. She wants to just have this time. She'll text her back when she gets home, around 7:00 p.m. As she is driving into town she notices how empty it is. Most people have left for the game. On the drive up to the house, no one is out. It feels good to be home, especially because no one is there and no one is coming.

When she walks into the house it is quiet and cold. "I can't wait to get out of this house," she thinks. No lights are on, no sounds, just an empty space. Sadie takes her bag upstairs and then comes down to fix something to drink. She sits down in the kitchen for a little while and then goes up to her room to watch TV.

# Chapter 26

It is a warm April day. The flowers have started to bloom. All of the trees are getting their leaves. The road is long and curved with budding trees arching over the road like a ceiling. The wind is lightly blowing, just enough to keep the heat down.

She is driving down the road remembering a time years before when she drove down this road. It seems like ages ago; she was a very young child. But she remembers. She remembers the road, she remembers the trees, but most of all she remembers why she is driving down that road.

The road is about 10 miles long and at the end of it is a great big colonial home, which is over 100 years old. In front of the house is a white sign which reads, "Grace's Sanatorium." It is a home straight out of the plantation days in the South. There are large porches off both sides of the front of the house. Above them are balconies covering the same area. The house is white with navy blue shutters. The porches and balconies are trimmed with white stone railings, still in great shape. Out front people sit in chairs that are randomly dispersed around the property. There is a large pond off to the right of the house. Ducks swim freely in the pond. There are several wooden benches along the bank.

As you walk inside the house to your right is a grand mahogany Cinderella staircase. It leads to a large landing at the top with three hallways; one to the right; one to the left; and one straight down the center. To the left of the door is a sitting area and to the right is a desk.

If you continue through the door into the house you will run into a locked door that shuts off access to the remainder of the home.

She walks up to the desk and signs in.

"Good morning Miss Mills, how are you today?"

"I'm good Stella. How are you?"

"I'm fine, thank you for asking."

She walks up to the locked door and Stella buzzes her in. She walks through the door into a long hallway. On either side of the hallway are doors as far as you can see. The hall is lined with fluorescent lights and looks an ugly shade of green, nothing like the facade you saw as you drove in. This is the inside of the home and it is weathered and worn. No expense is taken unless absolutely necessary.

She walks down, about half way, to Door 109. She stands outside for a moment, like she always did. When she turns the door knob to enter, she always expects a greeting but never gets one. She walks into the room and it is always the same. A bed, a table next to the bed and a chair. The curtains in the window are dingy white and not thick enough to keep even the dimmest light out. The bed is more like a cot; it doesn't move or adjust. It has one position. Flat. The room is stale, dingy and dark, completely depressing.

She walks over to the bed where the body of what seems to be a young girl lies. She is a tiny figure, wasting away. She can't weigh 80

259

pounds but she is still holding on, holding on for something no one understands.

She grabs her hand and sits on the bed next to her.

"Hi sweetie. How are you today? I know I haven't visited in a while but I have great news," she says as she starts to weep. She fights back her tears.

From behind her she hears, "What took you so long? I've been here for over an hour."

Sadie quickly turns around and sees her father Ed sitting in the chair in the corner behind the door.

"Hi Daddy. I'm sorry I was late, there was a lot of traffic." Sadie replies as if she's a five-year-old being disciplined by her father.

"Traffic huh! More like mourning over that prick of a husband of yours. The worst part about him getting shot is it wasn't by me!"

Sadie just sits silently holding Ellen's hand tight.

"I can't believe you fell for that piece of shit. You're a disgrace to this family, to Ellen!"

Sadie starts to sob, "I couldn't help it Daddy, and I tried. I mean, I did hate him at first but then it just started to fade. You don't know what it's like to have to get close to someone, be intimate with them when they've raped your sister!" Sadie face is expressionless, empty and pale. She puts her face in hands and cries.

"Fade. Maybe you should have come to see your sister more often and then it wouldn't have faded so fast."

"I didn't love him Daddy, I just...I just got used to him, I guess. It wasn't easy Daddy. You can't just make someone want to be with you. I had to work hard to get Mike to fall for me. It was confusing for me, Daddy! Don't you understand?"

"You're not making any sense, girl. It doesn't matter now, that crazy girl took care of it for us. With your money we can move your sister to a new place, a nicer place. You're getting the house and some of his money, right Sadie?"

Sadie is ignoring him. She's just starting to calm down until the images of Sarah shooting herself come rushing back.

"What are you crying for now, Sadie? You're just weak, weak!"

"She shot herself right in front of me Daddy. I thought she was gonna kill me, too!"

Joe walks over to Sadie and leans down to hug her, "I know, honey. I'm sorry. It's not your fault. You've done everything I've ever asked you to do. Now it's our turn. Our turn to live our lives."

"I love you, Daddy. You know that, right?" Sadie says, crying on Joe's shoulder.

"I know you do, honey. I love you, too. You've been a good daughter, done everything I asked you to."

There's a strange calm to Sadie's voice when she says, "We're finished; right, Daddy? The last one is done. It didn't go exactly as we wanted but it's done."

Joe ignores Sadie and turns to Ellen. "You would have been proud of us baby. Academy award winning performance by your sister! She was the perfect grieving girlfriend, shocked, angry; acting as if she was doing everything she could to fight back the tears. Really they were tears of joy, of joy for you, Ellen," his sarcasm is hard to miss. "Those bastards paid for what they did to you," he says angrily.

"Every day I remembered watching them, in the woods, rape and beat you. Sitting behind that tree crying as quietly as I could, knowing that if I tried to stop them they would do the same thing to me. I'm so sorry I didn't stop them, Ellen." Sadie weeps.

She is sobbing in her hands again. Sadie pauses for a moment; the tears are too much. Sadie remembers the look on Joe's face when she showed him Ellen in the woods. How he carried her in silence back to the house; cleaned her up and dressed her in new clothes. He worked so hard to move his family quietly from Blytheville. He truly believed Ellen would wake up…if they waited long enough.

Sadie looks at Ellen. Her face is vacant. She's just a vegetable staring into space? As Sadie looks at her she starts to get angry. How could those boys do this to a little girl?  Joe goes on with his story, very serious and calm.

He turns to Sadie, who is still very distressed.  "We spent a year studying poisons after Ellen's rape, Sadie.  Everything about them from what they are, how they work, to how to keep them from being traced.  It wasn't easy.  You really helped.  Remember, the first rule is a poison should be tasteless and odorless.  It can't have an effect in the target too early or too late, be slow acting or too fast.  The most important rule— untraceable, no one can know where you bought it.  Growing it ourselves was genius.  Absolute genius, Sadie.  Growing oleander, selenium and nectar from rhododendrons and azaleas.  They are all capable of decomposing in the body and are not easily detectable by an autopsy."  He pauses.  His tone gets very tense now.  He looks back to Ellen.

"The only bad thing about that girl shooting Mike is I wanted his parents to come to a place like this every day and watch their son wither away.  I wanted to show them what it feels like to be us, you lying in bed in a coma and me not being able to do anything.  You can't move, you can't speak, and you can't wake up.  You have no idea why you're here, but you are.  Now they all know.  They were in the prime of their life, just like you were.  We took it all away from them, just like they did to you."  Joe smiles as the words leave his mouth.

"Cyrus first, the ring leader, the director of it all."  Joe remembers.  "I enjoyed watching him persuade your sister to give him the pot she said she had found.  What an idiot.  It's interesting to watch someone and know it is only a matter of hours before they will be squirming for their life."

Sadie chuckled, remembering what she'd done. She didn't really understand what her dad was asking her to do but it was fun pretending. She was so young at the time.

"What idiot gets high before graduation?" Sadie says. Then she remembers John. She remembers watching him fight for Ellen. Just not hard enough, according to her dad.

"John didn't need to suffer," she heard herself say. She wished she could take the words back the second they left her mouth.

"What did you say?"

Sadie doesn't respond. She knows better.

"Spineless wimp. He didn't want to have sex with her but he didn't stop them either did he! Did he?" He yelled.

He took a deep breadth. "I followed you as you followed him to that coffee shop. He didn't even know you were there. You grabbed him a lid at the milk and sugar stand. He thought you were being helpful. He had no idea you were giving him a lid I dipped in poison." Joe says to Sadie. "I followed him to school after you left to head back up to Columbia. I watched what happened, Sadie. It didn't hurt for long, and he deserved it. They all deserved it. Even the parents!"

After a few seconds Sadie leans forwards and yells in Ellen's face, "Wake up! Why won't you wake up? I did this for you, aren't you happy?" Ellen does not respond, she is motionless. Sadie's eye's tear up and she takes a deep breadth.

"I still can't believe these guys never turned themselves in for what they did to you. If they would have, nothing would have happened to them. Especially Mike, the football star, and his wealthy parents." He turns to Sadie, "We had to do it, honey. Everything will be fine now. With that crazy girl shooting Mike they'll never connect the dots. Never tie it back to us. And now all his money is yours...ours. We can move Ellen to that nice hospital in Memphis that we always talked about. We couldn't have planned it better, Sadie, could we?"

Joe pauses for a moment. Brushes Ellen's cheek and smiles.

Sadie says, "So why don't I feel better?" Sadie gets up, wipes her eyes and puts Ellen's hand back under the blanket.

"Let's go, Sadie," her father orders. "We have more work to do!"

She and Joe came to the hospital separately but walk out of the hospital together.

Made in the USA
Lexington, KY
26 October 2010